The Princess Who Defied Kings

book one

A NOVEL BY

J. KIRSCH

White Phoenix Press

Printed in the United States of America

First Printing: September 2014

ISBN: 098864729X

ISBN-13: 978-0988647299

Praise for The Princess Who Defied Kings

One part heroic fantasy, one part snarky heroine with a mouth on her, one part adventure, one part romance. Add danger, a threat of mayhem and barely-escaped death, stir together and enjoy.
—K. G. McAbee, fantasy author and winner of the Black Orchid Award

FOR B.

Chapter 1

"Princess Najika of the White Kingdom, do you have anything to say for yourself?"

There was plenty I *wanted* to say. Not that it would do me any good. What did a girl say after killing her husband on their wedding night? Nothing I pointed out would justify what I'd done in the minds of the Law…Or those who carried it out.

"No, your Lordship. The condemned would only beg for the mercy of the Conclave." I bowed my head in modesty, though I felt anything but. My blood boiled and my mind seethed.

There were many Kingdoms, but they shared one Conclave, one Knight from each color who inherited artifacts of power and would pass them down to their sons, who would one day pass them to *their* sons, and so on until the eons yawned.

I remembered doing a lot of yawning when my father's lore keeper made me memorize the history of Arkor. Each Kingdom was named after a color, and my father was the White Knight, arguably the most powerful ruler of them all.

But as I looked across the echoing chamber of the court, I saw no pity in those eyes. Not even mercy. Father's distant gaze told me that I might as well have been a thief from the borderlands instead of his only daughter.

Kovinus the White, Kovinus the Fair. That's what others called the man I called Father. He'd always told me—*"Naji, I love you very much, but remember that for my Kingdom to prosper I must always value justice over mercy, and yes, even love. Never forget that. When I discipline you, it is for the good of all."*

We'd come a long way from that day when I was eight years old and stealing apples from the royal orchards. I wondered what he was feeling right now—not that it mattered. His sense of duty was sacrosanct. It wouldn't affect his decision. Not about me, not about anyone.

The Knights of all the other colors except for two sat in judgment of me, and in front of the high dais and all those ornately carved thrones stood a man who wore a shimmering cloak colored a cream that could blind eyes like the sun. He was a truthmaker, one of the men who prosecuted crimes at the Knights' court. He was the one who'd asked for my final remarks in his heavy, formal tone. I hated him for it, for how he drained my impending execution of any human element with his stiff-sounding words.

"May it please the Conclave, before you render judgment, I respectfully invoke the privilege of Recommendation *against* execution."

There was an uproar in the chamber. Murmurs erupted like squabbling geese, and my eyes snapped up to look at the man who had so far done everything in his power to paint my wretched guilt before everyone.

Jethred had one of those ageless faces carved in stone, and so I couldn't tell what the truthmaker had in mind, but I didn't think it could be good for me.

"Princess Najika has claimed extenuating circumstances…"

"Circumstances which we have only the word of a girl to corroborate," one of the Knights spat. My father stood up with a pained look.

"Truthmaker, what games do you play? We all know that a princess's words do not outrank an elder member of a Knight's family." He turned to face my mother-in-law who briefly was, the mother of the Red Knight. Her faded cheeks gathered with the heat of anger, and her hatred for me seemed to leap across the space, making my breath catch.

"The Lady Agwen has every right to wish justice for her son," my father continued, and though his eyes were filled with torment, they grew firmer by the moment. "This is what must be DONE," he thundered. "Who are you to invoke Recommendation in a case this heinous!?"

But Jethred didn't seem to bat an eye at Father's outburst. He calmly walked across the colorful mosaics on the tiles and stood toe to toe with him.

"Nonetheless I *do* invoke it, as is my *right*. And this is what I urge the Conclave to do. Take this princess and send her to wed the

Black Knight. Offer her as a peace offering that might one day bring the Black Kingdom into the fold with all the other Kingdoms of Arkor."

The ripples of whispers this time were more hushed. Chills made colonies of goose bumps along my arms and legs. I felt terror seize where my heartbeat should've been.

Father and the other Knights looked at him in shock. The Green Knight rose up, his gauntleted fingers slowly rubbing the stubble of his chin. He was known as the thoughtful Knight who seldom spoke. But he seemed intrigued by the certain, more cruel death which Jethred now dangled in front of the Conclave as my new fate.

"You propose giving the princess to the most feared and loathed man in existence. Never mind the fact that I *doubt* he would welcome a murderess into his marriage bed. Death by poisoning would be a gentler thing, wouldn't it? As the daughter of our brother Knight, she at least deserves that much consideration."

Since girlhood I had heard of the Black Knight's exploits. He was a sadist who supposedly killed, tormented, and raped purely for the enjoyment of it. No person had entered his realm and returned alive, except diplomats by his permission. In a few ages past one Knight or another had raised an army and tried his mettle by leading an invasion over the Black Kingdom's ragged ring of peaks. Shortly afterward, the son of a missing Knight would always be forced to take up his inheritance.

Only a few living people had ever even seen the Black Knight. He stood back, aloof from the world. Who knew—maybe he was as soft-hearted as a Kaledornian dwarf giving milk to a baby goat. But I seriously doubted it. I would never forget the one trip to the edge of that Kingdom, and what my Father had shown me—to 'educate' me, he'd said.

A line of skeletons, impaled skeletons…strung as far as the eye could see.

"Please, I beg you, don't do this." I was startled to realize that those words were coming out of *my* mouth.

"Why? Why this…Recommendation?" my father asked, excruciation returning to his eyes, aging his face right in front of me.

"What if the girl tells the truth? Consider it, lords," Jethred insisted. "If it is true, and Princess Najika killed the Red Knight with justification…" There were catcalls of outrage, but Jethred spoke over them.

"If the princess's story has any truth to it, then sending her into the Black Knight's Kingdom will at the very least serve a purpose of showing him our intent. Give him a letter, signed and sealed by the Conclave, informing him of her crime so that *he* can decide whether the princess is a vile murderess or whether she is redeemable by whatever twisted virtues he believes in."

He threw up his hands like a preacher haranguing his churchgoers. "We have tried to conquer the Black Knight through war, but no Knight has ever tried to use that other type of persuasion, my lords. The olive branch of peace might lead to trade. If it is worth the attempt, then doesn't offering the flesh and blood princess of one of our own Kingdoms—expendable and tarnished though she may be—make a powerful statement?"

Jethred whirled away from my father, now seeming to stare down the rest of the Conclave. Despite the embossed glory of each Knight in his suit of armor, somehow the finery of Jethred's cloak cowed them all. His demeanor subdued their doubtful expressions.

"And if she has lied about everything that led to the Red Knight's death, then that makes this fate only more appropriate."

Jethred turned to me, and a bony index finger pointed at me like I was a monster.

"Look at the fear in her eyes, lords. She has stood by quietly, displaying before us nothing but pride and stubbornness while I have outlined the evidence to her appalling act, the slaying of her own husband. Yet see now, there is fear. Real fear! I think she would gladly go to hang at the gallows…but this? This is another animal for her, my lords. You know it. So now I beg you, act on it. Follow my Recommendation. Let fate have its way with her."

When I'd looked down at Pordric's blood splattered everywhere—on the bed sheets, on my hands, my legs, my hips— then I'd known a second of fear. But it had subsided afterward because at least I'd known what to expect. But now? Robbed of the swift and merciful execution I'd anticipated, I found myself at a crossroads on the verge of torments I couldn't imagine.

One thing kept my spirits from collapsing though. It would be a long journey to the Black Kingdom. What opportunities would crop up on the way? Escape? A lucky encounter? I was not done yet, not by a long shot.

I had been disowned by Father, by everyone, but not by one important flame that seemed to flicker everlasting inside me. *Survive, Naji. Don't give up. You're a turnip that could grow on mountaintops, snow be damned.* My brother, were he here right now, would've told me that with a grin that said it was us against the world.

How I wished he were here now. I think he would have loved and supported me even after everything that had happened. I would do it for him. I would do it for me.

I would get away. I would be free.

Chapter 2

I'd made at least two friends on the endless journey. Three if you counted the dog who followed at a careful distance with curiosity. That was an accomplishment.

I walked on unsteady feet along with the rest of the banished prisoners. Though I was to be a 'wedding gift' for the Black Knight, the Conclave had decided by popular vote that I shouldn't be treated any differently.

Bereft of clothes, the other prisoners and I walked on the dirty, dusty road. My naked skin was caked with grime. I think even my eyelids had a fine layer of grit, the female prisoner's version of makeup.

Only two things made it bearable. There was a girl to my left and an elderly man to my right. We were all hitched to horses by our wrists, forced to stumble ahead at a pace just fast enough to induce the agony of fatigue. The girl was Bronwyn, and I couldn't remember the old man's name. But both could carry a tune, and as we plodded ahead their sparring voices took my mind off of the aches and burns which protested in one muscle after the next.

Oh, the Giant of Arkor, bearded was he.
He jumped over the Pearly Mountains and chuckled with glee
There he found mint cloves, and made he an ale
That made him so merry, he swam like a whale!

There were more verses and rhymes, most of them just as chock-full of nonsense, but Bronwyn told me that her brothers and sisters used to sing them in the fields to pass the time.

We were now ambling along the semi-paved, cough-creating 'road' through the Brown Kingdom. There was a long, flat plain on either side. Almost featureless. Boring. Of course boring could be good because each uphill shift made my legs burn with aches beyond aches.

I looked over at Bronwyn. She had tanned skin and callouses on her hands so unlike the soft skin along my palms and fingers. My bronze complexion might have fooled someone into thinking I was a hard worker, but the smoothness on my body up and down gave me away.

My feet were the one exception. They would be bleeding by the end of the day's march.

I wasn't looking forward to treating my blisters, let alone getting a good look at the ruins of my toes after the setting of the sun.

"Princess, it's an honor to walk next to you. I've never met royalty before, but now I can die a happy man. Who would've thought I would ever be marching next to a beauty like you?" The old man gave the kind of laugh that only a dirty old man on his last legs can get away with, but despite our mutual nakedness the comment didn't come across as offensive to me. His eyes never left my face, and there was a kindness in them that made me wish I could stare into them for a while instead of watching out for the next loose paving stone that might trip me and leave my arms or knees skinned to the bone.

Jorvi was the old man's name, *that* was it. It drifted down like a loose cobweb in my sweat-drenched head.

My dehydrated brain was by now moving in and out of clarity. My legs seemed to move automatically. The more numb they got, the less I cared what was ahead.

I vaguely ticked in my head how long we'd been traveling. Had it really been just over a week? What could I remember about the Brown Kingdom? Not much. I tried to stay alert, though. I made a valiant attempt to learn the words to some of the ridiculous songs Bronwyn and Jorvi started singing again.

That's when it happened. The first luck I could reach out and touch since my wedding night.

I remembered vaguely that the Brown Kingdom was less stable than the others. The Brown Knight was legendary for his laziness, and he didn't bother to police his realm all that carefully. Outlaws, brigands, highwaymen—let's just call them 'bandits' to make it simple—multiplied in the forests which pockmarked the plains here and there like tufts of fur.

We had just started down a sudden dip in the road, and we kept going along to where the road must have been paved through the eye of a ravine. Whatever river had scoured out the ravine was long gone, but the trees here had seen it all. They were thicker than the tower outposts along the borders of the White Kingdom, their glistening red bark taunting me to touch them.

I was just trying to focus back on the road when I heard a twig snap. And then it dawned on me that the 'twig' was actually a large branch swinging out onto the road at hurtling speed. The branch was wide, long, and spiked with vicious wooden stakes. These same stakes now skewered several lightly armored guards at the front of our column. Arrows whispered from the shadows of the trees, driving home into pink flesh. A grizzled old warden in a chainmail shirt cried out as his neck sprouted a red-feathered shaft.

He toppled over, groaning as I stepped over him, praying for his suffering to be long and agonizing. Vicious? Maybe, but after seeing his butt undulate back and forth in comfort on the horse which forced me to march at a stumbling trot day after day, I'd stoked a good deal of hate for the man.

I gave in to instinct, and before anyone realized what was happening I had run forward, ignoring the needles in my feet and jumping awkwardly up onto the saddle. With my wrists bound in front of me I couldn't maneuver very well. I hung over the horse like a sack of potatoes for several heart-pounding moments, nearly falling headfirst onto the road before my fingers found a grasp on the stirrup.

I swung about, carefully shifting my weight and letting my feet settle in. There was a lot of slack rope which connected my bound wrists to the pommel of the saddle, but other than being an annoyance it didn't prevent me from doing what I needed to do next.

I should've just ridden into the forest and thrown the dice, but I didn't. *You're not leaving them, Naji. You're not.* I turned and nudged my nervous horse onto a collision course with the armored guard riding the horse in front of Bronwyn. The guard's attention was distracted. He had his shield raised, and four lethal shafts had already embedded themselves in the wood. He was bellowing to some of his brothers in arms when my horse collided into him just hard enough to disorient him. I reached over, grasping the hilt of a knife at his belt. I drew it and plunged it into the unprotected flesh of his thigh.

That's the thing about long journeys in hot weather—guards don't like to sweat, and they don't always wear armor head to foot. I jerked backward just in time to avoid the wild cut of his blade. His shield arm dipped for just a moment as he howled in pain, and that was all it took for the next shaft to whoosh past his defenses, finding a gap between the breastplate and the arm guard. The armored warden grunted in pain and tried to kick his mount into a gallop to get himself clear of the battle.

Yes, and if he does that he'll reduce your friend's body to a bloody pulp as she bounces along the ground behind him. Hearing the terror in Bronwyn's cry must've given me equal parts strength and courage because somehow I launched myself at the guard, and the crown of my skull met his chin with a violent crack.

I felt something in his jaw give way as we both toppled over his horse. He hit the ground and I didn't. The rope from my wrists went taut, and I probably would've broken both hands if Bronwyn hadn't rushed to my side, her hands cradling my shoulders and pushing me back up until I could pivot astride the horse she was still bound to.

"Let's switch horses," I said. "Follow me." I tried to say it like I knew what I was doing. Bronwyn looked hardier than me, but I could be decisive when I wanted to be, and the hesitation in her eyes told me that she…not so much.

Jorvi was gone. The scene behind us had deteriorated into a chaos of ragged, unwashed bodies and armored ones, the ring of sword against sword, and horses crying out in pain. I saw one gap-toothed bandit bring down an axe the length of his whole body onto the head of an unsuspecting guard from behind.

The guard's head…it was like a melon which…My mind tried to blot it from memory, and I turned back to what mattered. Survival.

Chapter 3

The outlaws probably didn't have a chance, *that much* the periphery of my vision could tell me. I had to give them credit for an ambush well executed, but our escort to the Black Kingdom included one of the Knights of the Conclave. The Blue Knight, Sir Gewthur, was not much older than me, but he cut a dashing figure in his sapphire-glossed armor. Like any good artifact of power, the blue armor had special traits. The lore keeper's annoying lessons reminded me that it protected the wearer from heat, cold, not to mention the bite of any axe, blade, or arrow point.

I threw one last look over my shoulder. Curiosity sometimes got the best of me, even when I shouldn't have let it. Like a man who thought that the rest of the world was made up of butter with him as the appointed knife, Gewthur was slashing his way through a wave of outlaws, hacking joyfully and rallying the guards to him like the beacon of death-dealing he was.

Wait to get recaptured or plunge into the unknown. Not a hard choice, Naji. Bronwyn and I forced our horses under the canopied shadows of the trees and kept our horses at a steady but not grueling pace. It wouldn't do much good to have one of the horses stumble and throw us clear of the saddle. A good way to break bones, ours or the unfortunate beasts we rode, but not good if we wanted to have even a hope of escaping.

As the ground sloped up again the sounds of battle faded behind us. We continued at a brisk yet not killing rhythm until our horses cleared the trees. Then we were off, the hooves of our mounts pummeling the earth beneath us as the wind caressed my cheeks with the first teases of freedom.

You can't celebrate when you're dead, Naji. My brother's sobering saying intruded on my brief spell of happiness. Naked on a horse with no provisions and one equally handicapped companion was no condition to brag about, let alone celebrate. I tried to look around and get my bearings. Luckily Bronwym seemed to know her way around a horse. The animal already had relaxed noticeably, same for mine, and neither of our four-legged friends were the worse for wear. We rode them hard, though, and by the time the sun was dipping behind the distant horizon there was labored breathing from our entire party, two-legged and four-legged beings now equally exhausted.

"Have we lost them?" Bronwyn asked, her chest heaving as she pulled her reins up beside me.

I gave her a grim smile. "Ask me that in another week if we aren't bird food." I looked at the distant sky where vultures circled, their wingspans as wide as a horse was long. They'd eat a hearty meal tonight, and I wanted to be as far from that meal as humanly possible.

We stumbled along in the fading light until things started to get ridiculous. Breaking a horse's leg would seal our fate, and the benefit of an extra few feet of space between us and our pursuers wasn't worth the risk. I motioned at a clump of trees. They were big, mature oaks with outspread branches. I maneuvered my horse between them, jumped down and looked for something, anything sharp and gray. I finally found a decent-sized rock, just slightly bigger than my fist. It had a jagged edge. Although it took me forever to get the rock wedged between some roots and propped at the proper angle, I finally got it to where I could rub my bound wrists across the edge at a nice, even pace.

It took me a while, sweat pouring into my eyes. Bronwyn watched my progress greedily after she'd sampled several worthless rocks too smooth for her purposes. Just then the sky blurted out thunder, its echoing booms oddly comforting to me as the rope, worn ragged on my wrists, finally tore through.

"Infinitely better," I muttered, rubbing my raw skin. I turned and held the rock extra steady for Bronwyn, which made her process go by that much quicker than mine had. With a sparkling smile she raised up both hands in triumph once the cords snapped apart.

"Now what?" Bronwyn said, looking around uneasily as the thunder boomed again, the sound moving closer.

A light rain began to fall. I couldn't help myself, and I grinned, opening my mouth to drink up the drops. I motioned toward where the trees were thickest, and we maneuvered our way over, managing to find a dry place despite everything. We let the horses wander a little. I had a lot of experience riding them, but caring for them had always been the servant's duty.

Fortunately Bronwyn seemed to have the experience I lacked. She showed me how best to tend to the beasts, and we ended up huddling together with them to wait out the storm. I leaned against a dry tree trunk with Bronwyn's body pressed against mine, our warmth surprisingly good as the temperature plummeted through the night. We'd taken a blanket from the saddlebags since it was the only clothing we had, and in no time we had ourselves cocooned in it.

Given some time Bronwyn said she could make us some decent clothing. We did have tools, after all. Knives. Other odds and ends.

As we sat huddled at the base of the tree, our blanket snugly wrapped to encase us in the best warmth I'd ever felt, I found at one point that I couldn't go back to sleep. Bronwyn's breathing didn't sound as deep as it had earlier, so I risked giving her a jostle with my elbow.

"You awake?"

"If I wasn't before, I am now," she replied. She looked over at me then, and her weak attempt at humor evaporated.

"Princess Najika, I'm scared. What are we going to do?"

"First off, you aren't going to call me 'Princess' ever again. Call me Naji."

The blond girl gave me an apologetic look, but the terror in her eyes hadn't lessened one bit.

"Secondly, we take this one day at a time. Every day we stay a step ahead of Sir Gewthur, that ups our chances of them giving up and turning back, right?"

Bronwyn gave me a slightly reassured nod. Okay…now to reel her in.

"More importantly, for all we know the bandits killed most of them. Sir Gewthur may be strong, but he's still just one man. If he doesn't have the support he won't keep coming after us." That last part was probably wishful thinking. If he went back without us he would probably need some evidence that we had died in the wilderness. To do anything else would make him the dishonored laughingstock of the Conclave. No, the more I thought about it, the more I understood that the Blue Knight would probably not give up unless things became extremely desperate.

Fear niggled at the back of my mind. I needed to change my frame of thinking, and fast.

Something rustled in the bushes. We both tensed as a hooded figure leapt out of the shadows. In the flash of moonlight dappling between two branches all I could see was that he had an eye patch and a dagger glinting in his hand.

Eye-patch was on us before I could move, and he pressed a blade to my throat.

"Well, if'n it isn't two lonely ladies out in the woods on a dark and stormy night. May curses rain on the Boss's head. He said it'd be *easy*. Easy, queasy says I! Pick up a few slaves and be on with things, take 'em to market out in the Great Woods where the cruel Knights and their mindless little soldiers don't come'n ruin our fun." One-Eye's speech was slurred, and that was when I noticed that some kind of trauma to his face had left him permanently disfigured.

He leered at us, sizing us up despite the fact that only the tops of our slim shoulders and faces were visible above the blanket. He should've been paying more attention because I used that flimsy distraction to maximum benefit, ramming my knee upward into his groin area.

The bandit made a gurgling sound which rapidly died off when my second kneecap thrust connected with the side of his head. The pain lancing up my leg was worth it. He soon lay at our feet looking almost peacefully asleep with his tongue lolling from his half-open mouth.

Brownyn looked at me, aghast. "Is he…?"

"Dead? No," I said with disappointment.

"If he caught up to us, though, it probably means that our pursuers can't be far behind."

I nodded in agreement with Bronwyn, but what else could we do? We could walk on foot in the night, but all that would accomplish would be to make our feet totally useless by morning, assuming we didn't become hopelessly lost and disoriented. Judging from the character of the bandit, he seemed the cowardly sort. He'd probably run at the start of the battle, which meant that maybe, just maybe, we were clear of most of the men, bandits and guards.

Still, I didn't want to count on it. There were a lot of things I didn't want to have to count on, luck being one of them. But fallen princesses couldn't be choosers, so...

I tried to remember Gewthur's reputation. What would he be *likeliest* to do? He was a vain young stud—my father's words, not mine. Once he set his mind on something, he was known to be obsessive. I thought back to whispered words between my parents when I was young, something about one of the servants addicted to a certain 'medicinal' herb. That was the kind of obsessive addiction I imagined was part of the Blue Knight's personality.

"I think..." I chewed on my lip as the thought fully formed. "I wouldn't be surprised if Gewthur spent the entire night trying to gain ground on us. He's probably furious that we escaped. He's young and impetuous, probably willing to take risks where an older Knight would be patient."

Bronwyn and I talked between ourselves about the few options we did have, and the solution we came up with was an unconventional one to say the least.

***

They found us at dawn. Gewthur and his men, bone-weary, finally discovered our two shivering forms at the foot of the oak trees. The Blue Knight looked down on us, his breathing ragged, and raised the visor of his helm.

"Do not attempt to flee."

"Does it look like we're in any condition to flee?" I said, and then I pointed to One-Eye tied up and gagged a stone's throw away. "We tied that one up for you to bag, our way of contributing to the greater good. Will you have some mercy on us at least? We can hardly walk." I turned up my feet, revealing the puckered skin and blister-filled geography from my soles to my toes.

The Blue Knight looked at us with a glimmer of concern. At the outset of the journey he had cared only about efficiency. As long as we were still breathing, he'd pointed out, that was what mattered.

Despite the fatigue clearly setting in, though, Gewthur seemed more ready to sympathize. It was as if his own body's pains were making him more aware of others' hurts. He sighed, as if we were two sisters refusing to play his favorite game.

"You can rest. Fine."

"And bathe. There has to be a spring near here. We heard loud splashing when our horses wandered off earlier this morning." I waited to see if my bold demand would gain any traction. To my surprise the Blue Knight nodded. Given the signs so far, I decided to push my luck.

The next thing I tried I did out of desperation. Although I regretted it even as I did it, this was still part of the plan, and I couldn't let fear rule me now.

I dropped the blanket and boldly walked up to the Knight, putting my hands softly against the hard breastplate of his armor. "Perhaps you would let me show my appreciation for your kindness in letting us rest?" I gave him what I hoped was an alluring look. I imagined what he was seeing—the curve of my breasts, the shoulder-length, raven black hair which probably looked just about as disheveled as a bird's nest. Some guys find that sort of thing sexy, and more than a few are idiots. I calculated how much armor he would have to strip off in order for me to incapacitate him with a shot to the groin or a finger-stab to the eye sockets if my main hope failed.

Meanwhile his men were so exhausted they'd practically fallen to the ground wherever they could find a flat space the moment after we'd been found. The Blue Knight had been driving them hard throughout the night. After fighting bandits and watching many of their friends die, they were at the end of their stamina and it showed. I'd never seen so many men fall asleep almost instantly.

The Blue Knight seemed to look longingly at me, tantalized by my offer. His gauntleted hands curved to my rear, and I mentally prepared to strike like the pet snake my father had sometimes let me feed rabbits to. I let him go so far as to put his visor up higher, tipping my mouth upward as our lips joined for a tentative kiss. I deepened the kiss, and my plan soon reached the critical point.

Just a few more heartbeats, Naji. He drew back abruptly a few seconds later, frowning at me.

"My fatigue must be clouding my wits. If you could slay Pordric, my Red Knight brother, I shudder to think what you would do to me. Gorgeous as you are, I don't think I'm willing to lose my life for a false promise, no matter how…tempting."

I looked at the Knight with a sad smile. The fool didn't realize that I'd dabbed poison on my lips from one of the vials in One-Eye's pouch.

Bandits loved coating their weapons in poison since it tended to even the odds against a better armored foe, and it didn't hurt a girl to adapt that to her own purposes. The only question was…how long would it take to circulate though the Blue Knight's body, and how severe would the reaction be? Would it be enough to kill him?

The Blue Knight's body jerked as if replying to the unspoken thoughts in my mind. Gewthur opened his mouth, but no sound came out. He clawed at his throat as if the airway there wasn't wide enough.

I looked back at Bronwyn, who had already quietly started preparing the horses. She gave me a hand up. We had just urged our mounts forward when the first cry of alarm went up from one of the guards. I looked back just in time to see four men crashing towards us. I wanted to get the horses moving, but we weren't clear of the oak trees. I panicked, kicking the horse into a gallop with the space still too tight.

A leafy tree branch swatted me out of the saddle like a fly, and I lay dazed with Bronwyn screaming my name.

"Naji! Get up, now! We have to GO!" I looked up in time to see the first of four men reach me. He had a ring through his nose, and his eyes were a dead grey, sort of like ash. He grabbed me by my hair, lifting me up with rage in his eyes. My scalp stung and my eyes watered, but I tried to focus.

"You've killed him, you stupid—" He probably meant to say more, none of it complimentary, but you don't mess with a lady's hair, and especially a princess's. I head-butted him in the nose, which I think came as a surprise to him because I probably had to sacrifice a few strands of hair in the process.

The dazed look in his eyes and the proximity of the next three onrushing figures told me that I had maybe five heartbeats to start getting mobile or who knew what these guys would do to me. If the Blue Knight really did die from the poison, I seriously doubted that these men would escort me the rest of the way to my appointed date with death or torture at the Black Knight's hands.

So I did the only thing I could do. I ran and then I leapt. There was no time for me to jump onto my own horse because it had wandered too far after the branch-swatting fiasco. But Bronwyn had wheeled her horse back around and brought it close, and now I easily jumped up behind her and screamed for her to move like lightning.

"Hold on!" she cried, and we did just that—the horse zigzagging through the thinning trees until we were back out on the open grasslands, a swaying canvas which seemed to beckon toward more freedom on the horizon. That was when I heard a second set of hooves drumming the ground behind us, and I turned back with a sinking feeling.

The guard I'd head-butted had regained his senses, and what was more, he'd hopped onto my horse and spurred it into a full gallop. In the distance I could see more guards who'd finally recovered senses lost during their brief beauty sleep, and they were now bearing down on us from several angles.

Seven pursuers in all, including the hair-grabbing maniac who was hot on our trail. My heart ricocheted inside my ribcage. I didn't see us getting out of this one. I shuddered at the thought of what these men might do to us. At the moment, though, I was just grateful that Bronwyn seemed to be holding it together. No, she was doing better than that. She was all business, her focus all on the terrain ahead of us, threading one treacherous gap to the next and then the next.

The chase became a test of endurance. Whose horse would tire first? Fortunately six of the guards seemed to have taken particularly poor care of their mounts in recent days. Riding them all night probably hadn't helped either. Gradually they became fuzzy, less distinct figures as we glanced back, but the hair-grabbing guard with the enraged eyes was a thorn we couldn't quite shake.

He was getting very close now. The sun glinted against his chainmail as he drew his blade with a flourish. His teeth clenched with anticipation, triumph—the joy of an impending kill lighting up his eyes. I was clinging to Bronwyn for dear life, praying for a miracle. I didn't get one, at least not in the way I hoped.

A spear leapt through the air, punched through cartilage and bone right between the guard's eyes. At the same time I felt an incredible wall of force, my neck feeling the whiplash as a net enfolded us between two trees. The horse whinnied and thrashed, which only further ensnared us as the net tangled in my hair. I screamed as the horse bucked, forcing me and Bronwyn to slip clear of the saddle. Then the stomping hooves were a dangerous hand's width from our prone bodies as the beast continued to panic, its nostrils flaring.

Getting stomped to death by a frightened animal wasn't how I'd envisioned my life ending, and I twisted desperately, trying to carve out a pocket in the net and somehow separate me and Bronwyn from the whirling hooves of death. My eyes widened in horror as I saw another spear impale the horse through the side, but at least its struggles tapered off and the bone-crushing hooves stopped flailing. I hugged Bronwyn tightly, tears slipping down my face as I told her, "SSHHH. It's okay. They're not guards. We're going to be okay."

The truth was, whoever had captured us, they could be anyone, worse than the guards for all I knew. I wracked my brain for which Kingdoms bordered the Brown Kingdom.

I remembered slowly, the colors gliding into my mind. *Yellow.* *Green. Black.* I froze as shapes, each enshrouded with loose-fitting ashen wraps, huddled eagerly around our prone bodies. We lay in the grass, just panting, clinging to each other. I looked into Bronwyn's blue eyes, strangely distracted by how beautiful they were even in her fear.

Of all the stupid things to fixate on, Naji. If these are going to be your last moments on earth, at least make them count.

I diverted my attention, noticing that the hooded faces peering at us were covered. They had on masks which were not normal at all, almost insanely disproportionate. The masks protruded outward with long, hooked noses and gaping slits for eyes. Yes, the eyes behind those masks were *huge*. They couldn't be human.

"Just let me die." That was all I could mutter under my breath as hands reached out to untangle us from the netting, and I closed my eyes.

Chapter 4

They practically danced as they walked, and even when standing or sitting still, they always seemed on the verge of motion. We sat in the center of their encampment, wondering what exactly they intended to do with us.

I tried to recall the jumble of what had happened beginning from when they'd snared us in their net. I remembered many arms untangling me, lifting me up, carrying me and then tipping me onto my feet. An old woman tried to communicate, but her words were elegant gibberish to me. She handed me something to drink. Though it smelled foul, it tasted surprisingly good. Watery with a hint of sweetness.

We were surrounded by a bustle of activity as they went about preparations, and for what I didn't know, but the real question niggling at me came down to this...Who were they?

The people who'd captured Bronwyn and me were unlike any *I'd* ever seen. Their legs seemed to have joints in odd places, and they could run faster than I could ever hope to run. They dressed funny too, in flowing wraps that reminded me of someone coiled up in five sets of bed sheets. How it all stayed together and didn't fall around their ankles was a mystifying puzzle. Or at least would have been if I didn't have more worrisome things on my mind.

I had trouble looking at their faces. Those creepy masks still made my blood run cold. But their actions seemed to speak louder than their creepiness.

Two of the strange people approached us and indicated that we were to follow. Normally I didn't blindly follow creatures wearing hideous masks who'd just snared me in some kind of trap. But the neatly folded clothing in each one's hands seemed to indicate that they intended to let us actually wear something, and that thought sent tingles of joy up and down my spine.

I motioned at Bronwyn with a sort of 'These people may not be completely crazy, so let's see what they want,' waggle of the eyebrows, and she nodded readily enough.

Most of the encampment sat at the bottom of a hill, so we had to walk around as we followed our two guides. I started to hear the trickle of water, and then it sounded more like a flood. We rounded the bump of the hill and I gasped at the rocky ridge that sort of thrust out of the earth like a dirty fingernail. Beyond it were hills that stepped up and up toward snow-sparkly mountains, but the nearby waterfall had my attention. I longed for those cascading veils of precious liquid to caress my mud-caked, grimy skin.

"May we?" I said, indicating the waterfall and the placid pool that was nature's version of a bath tub.

The strange people—and for some reason I thought they were female—gently set down our clothes, and I realized that a third one had been following us. He kept us at a distance, but quietly set down two lengths of drying cloth and tossed us what looked like soap. The stuff smelled foul, but I smiled and said, "We will go wash up. Thank you." Could they even understand a word I was saying?

The water was cold, but not as cold as it might've been. It was well past dawn and the day promised to be a scorcher. The coolness of the water was already a comforting contrast on my skin. Bronwyn laughed as I splashed her, but my eyes were serious. I kept splashing her with water for a while longer, and smiled when she splashed back. If we were being closely watched, I didn't want our hosts thinking that we were up to something. I was all business now as we splashed and soaped ourselves back to smelling like honest-to-goodness human beings.

"Do you have a place you want to get to?" I asked her.

She seemed confused by the bluntness of what I'd asked. "I don't know what you mean, Prin—Naji…" She sighed, her eyes clouding over. "I can't go back to my family. I have nowhere to call home. If these things treat us decently, I might be willing to stay with them."

She looked at me, her eyes searching my face for something they couldn't find. "I see you're not in the same boat though," Bronwyn said.

"Look, whoever these creatures are, I doubt they speak our language. I don't trust them. I don't trust anyone." *Except for you.* Those words almost slipped from my lips. It was so weird. Two weeks ago we'd never even met. And yet the insane odyssey of the past seven or eight days had sealed a bond between us. She wasn't just a fellow prisoner anymore. She was the sister I'd never had.

"You present somewhat of a problem for me though," I went on. I decided she needed to know that I was willing to go with her on this, that I *wouldn't* abandon her. I gave her a fierce hug, the kind you give someone you haven't seen in a year or two.

"Naji, what are you going to do?"

"For one thing, I'm not leaving you. We're in this together. Got it?" I gave her a cross look, but it melted like sunbathed butter when she returned my hug with a squeeze every bit as tight.

"Okay. So what's our plan? We need a plan, right? How do we go about trying to communicate?"

I was just about to respond to that when a tingling sensation of recognition surged through my torso. I had that feeling of suddenly being intently watched, and when I turned he took my breath away.

"No. It can't be." I saw the dark horns protruding from his helm, and the wide backing of the helm flared outward, making his face seem twice as menacing. He didn't wear metal armor like I'd seen the other Knights wear on special occasions or when Father had taken me on his travels.

The Black Knight wore a tight-fitting piece of body armor, and it wasn't made of any material I recognized. It seemed more flexible than leather, but also sturdier too, if that made any sense. Cleary I was no armorer, but the weapons and armor part of my studies with Father's boring tutors had been one of the few lessons I had actually *paid attention to*.

He beckoned us with his hand, and my heart beat out a frantic rhythm in my chest even as the water temperature seemed to plunge. Bronwyn took my hand. "We stick together, Naji." She gave me a brave look and nudged us both forward. I was supposed to be the one doing that, not her, but I gratefully took the courage that seemed to flow from her intertwining fingers through mine.

"I think it's safe to say that those mountains in the distance are the border to the Black Knight's Kingdom," I said dryly as we waded through the pool towards shore.

"At least we have a better geographical feel for where we are," Bronwyn replied. She was trying for optimism, but we both knew that she was trying way too hard. I gave her trembling hand a 'SSHH, it'll be okay' squeeze even though it probably wouldn't.

We finally stopped before the Black Knight, our waists and legs still in the water. The two-handed sword strapped to his back loomed like a snake ready to strike us. A coiled dragon with ruby-set eyes perched on the pommel of the great-sword, its fangs bared. It sent a shiver down my torso, between my breasts, all the way to my core.

The Black Knight regarded us steadily, and it seemed as if even the waterfall and the birdsong in the trees were hushing themselves, waiting for him to speak.

"So. Is this my bride-to-be?" He gave me a rough glance, his eyes giving my figure a soft caress. "It doesn't seem fair, Lady Najika. Here you are naked and I am fully clothed. If we are to wed, at least you should have a measure of me and decide if I'm worthy of your hand. Don't you think?"

Having said those words, the Black Knight appalled me by removing his armor and then his clothes. He laid the sheathed great-sword lovingly on the ground and waded into the water, dipping his head under and coming up with a glistening mantle of charcoal-black hair above blue eyes which crinkled with warmth. I was stunned.

"Forgive me. Your beauty distracted me and I seem to have forgotten my manners. My full name is Drakonius Vezinor, but I think we can both agree that's too much of a mouthful. My friends call me Drake."

He extended a hand politely to me. Fortunately the water level covered him up to the waist. Of course that didn't hide the rugged, mountain-like handsomeness of his face, the amusement in his eyes, or the patterns of muscles clearly visible across his chest. I tried to swallow.

"Pleasure to meet you," I said, giving his hand a quick shake before drawing my hand back. As he shook Bronwyn's hand and said a few kind things to her, my body tensed. My mind screamed at me to shift into higher alertness.

This is the man who is known as a monster throughout Arkor. The man who lines his borders with a string of impaled skeletons stretching for miles. Whatever he appears to be on the outside, don't you dare trust it, Naji.

But my instincts said something very different than the paranoia raging in my head. My muscles relaxed being around this man. I felt safe standing almost next to him despite the circumstances, despite everything I'd heard. There was no malice in those eyes. Desire, yes, but even that was harnessed and controlled. He turned away, and I saw the giant dragon tattoo which covered the whole of his back. The dragon had four outstretched talons, as if it were preparing to descend on something and rake out the eyes of its prey.

"Do you like it?" he asked.

"It's certainly unique." Bronwyn and I exchanged an uncertain look.

"It's the artifact of power that keeps my Kingdom whole. I bet you didn't expect to hear that," he said with a laugh, turning back to face me.

He must've seen the confusion in my eyes. "Everyone knows the stories of course. I'm assuming you know the legend of how Arkor supposedly began?"

I gave him a thin glare. "I never liked history lessons as a child, and I certainly don't like them any better now," I huffed. "Yes,

Black Knight, I know the history of Arkor. Thousands and thousands of years ago…blah, blah, blah, the land was filled with a bunch of antisocial tribes who killed each other and even ate human flesh. People treated each other like animals before the coming of King Artur and his Magician. Artur and his Magician cowed the tribe-lords and made them bow before him. He created his Knights of the Round Table, giving to each reformed leader certain artifacts of power to maintain his own Kingdom and preserve it for his descendants. Within a few decades Artur and his Magician vanished, never to be seen again. We all know the story. My own father, the White Knight, traces his lineage all the way back to that time."

The Black Knight clapped. "Bravo. You're very succinct. And feisty. I like that."

He waded towards me, his hand reaching out to snake mine into his grasp. I began to pull away, but the look in his eyes stopped me.

"The tattoo on my back has magical properties. It allows me to see through the eyes of people whom I trust. I have spies everywhere, Princess. I have to, because my enemies are many. One of my spies was in the household of the Red Knight on your wedding night, and through her I know what really happened."

My body stiffened and my hand clenched inside his. I tried to focus on the enfolding warmth of his fingers as the fear and shame threatened to erupt through my chest.

"I know as well as you do that what happened that night was not your fault. You didn't know that the man you were to marry was a monster. Your instincts suspected it, though, didn't they?" His softened gaze seemed to plead for my honesty, and my troubled eyes managed to meet his without flinching.

"How can you know this?" I said.

"I just told you how," he replied simply.

"Yes, and I need time to absorb it, thank you very much!" My cheeks went hot, and I didn't know whether to laugh or to cry at the strangeness of the situation. My emotions were running hot and cold.

I shuddered, and he put his other hand on top of our enfolded ones. Other than that he stood still, not trying to touch me.

"I understand, Princess. You have been through quite a lot in a very short amount of time. After you finish bathing I will give you and Bronwyn a few hours to rest, but then we must talk and a decision must be made, and the decision can't be made by me. It must be yours."

He let go of my hand and turned to swim to the other side of the pool to give us our privacy.

"Wait." I gave him a sharp look. "Tell me why? Why did you tell me that just now?"

"Because I want you to feel safe. I know that you are *not* a murderess. You are safe here with my allies and with me. For now, although I understand you can't fully trust me, I hope that's enough." He turned and dove under the water, his feet kicking as his body made an appealing figure slicing through the pool towards the opposite side.

He seemed to be content washing and soaping himself apart, giving us our privacy. Bronwyn and I finished our bathing in silence, gathered up the clothes we were given and tried them on. The tunic and trousers fit me perfectly and were a beautiful black with gold thread. A phoenix's wings spread from one armpit to the other across the front. The moment I put it on I felt strangely calm. And safe. The anxiety and hurt inside me seemed to drain away to some forgotten place.

The same two people with the big-nosed masks who'd led us to the bathing pool now showed us back to camp, leaving us at a tent which they indicated was ours using a series of gestures and guttural sounds.

I stepped inside with a sigh of relief when I saw a decent place to lay down for a nap. I'd been chased and nearly killed by guards and bandits. I had every right to be exhausted, and my body was getting insistent about this foreign concept called 'sleep.'

"Naji, are you okay?"

"I'm not sure what okay would even mean at this point," I replied with a shudder. I looked around at the tent to see what other objects we'd been given.

"What decision was he talking about?"

I gave Bronwyn an annoyed look. "How should I know? If I had to guess, I'd say that it has something to do with me marrying him."

"You're not considering it, are you Naji? I know he's not the Black Knight you expected to find," Bronwyn said, and for some reason I wanted to smack her.

My gaze drifted over to the various items laid out on the sleeping pallet. I frowned, shocked at what I saw. A sword's tip winked at me, the sun's light catching it through the tent's opening. The scabbard next to it was embroidered with purple amethysts down one side and glacier-blue sapphires up the other. There was also a bow of sturdy wood with a quiver of iron-tipped arrows perched in the corner. Assorted daggers and a belt of throwing knives were strung out like the Black Knight's strange version of jewelry.

I moved the weapons aside and laid down on the pallet, closing my eyes and trying to find some sort of inner peace. I hadn't had a good night's sleep in several weeks, and the fatigue settled into my brain, numbing me and preparing me for unconsciousness.

"We're clothed and armed. Naji, should we try to find a way to escape?" I opened one eye and looked at her. Bronwyn meant well. I knew she did. But right now she was just making things worse.

"Bronwyn, I'm exhausted. If the Black Knight didn't have plans to make sure we couldn't escape, I don't think he would've given us all these weapons. What I need right now is time to think and to rest. Besides, weren't you the one who was entertaining the idea of staying with these people?"

Bronwyn gave me a pitying look. "That was before I knew they were in league with the Black Knight! I wouldn't wish to see you forced to marry that monster."

I appreciated her kindness and concern, but right now my head was spinning and I needed rest before I could make my next move, whatever that move turned out to be.

"He did not sound like a monster, Bronwyn. Besides, I've already married and killed one monster. What's one more?" I replied with morbid humor, turning over and closing my eyes, begging for sleep. It claimed me even sooner than I'd expected, and I heard Bronwyn lay down beside me.

Chapter 5

I awoke refreshed, my body singing with new energy. It was like this nap had not only refreshed me, but rebirthed me.

Careful there, Princess. Remember you're at the mercy of the Black Knight, was what my paranoid voice so generously reminded me.

Bronwyn was still fast asleep, but I heard footsteps approaching the tent. I took my sword and stepped to the side of the tent flap, waiting. Something about the sound of the footsteps made me think that it would be the Black Knight himself, and I wasn't disappointed.

As he stepped through I slid the blade up, pressing the point against his throat as he put up both hands.

"You can release us or die. Those are your choices," I whispered.

"Is this how they say 'hello' in the White Kingdom?"

Like any princess raised in Arkor, I'd been trained to fight with sword and bow, plus a half dozen other weapons besides. The Knights raised both their daughters and sons to be practical champions to protect their Kingdoms, and I'd been no exception.

"You'll find I'm quite good with a blade, Black Knight. I wouldn't recommend arguing. You'll come along as our bound hostage and once we're at a safe distance I'll let you go free," I said, my muscles tense. One move and I'd skewer his throat like a cucumber.

"Call me Drake. It's my name, Princess."

"Lovely," I replied, my voice dripping sarcasm. "Call me Naji. You might as well know the name of the girl who's about to run you through."

He realized that despite the sarcasm I was deadly serious. His eyes found mine and worked their annoying, beseeching magic. Suddenly I felt like an ungrateful guest rather than a desperate captive who needed her freedom.

By now Bronwyn was awake. To her credit she'd picked up her own sword and stood ready to back me up if the Black Knight made any sudden moves.

"I appreciate your fear and distrust, Naji. Truly I do. But I'm not here to hurt you, and actually quite the opposite. You have a decision to make, and depending on what you decide the trolls will either fight for you or not. Please, put down the weapon so that we can talk."

Wait. Did he just say 'trolls'?

"Trolls?" I lowered my weapon, completely baffled. Bronwyn did the same, and we both gaped at him.

The Black Knight beckoned us out of the tent, and as we followed he swept his arm around the encampment where tall, disjointed shapes bustled this way and that wearing their funny-looking wraps of clothing and big-nosed, huge-eyed masks.

"You didn't think these people were actually human, did you?" Drake said, looking at me with a touch of mirth.

"I…didn't know what to think," I finished lamely. Damn him, but he actually smiled at me.

"I must admit, you look very cute when you're confused. You might just make a fetching bride after all." He carefully stepped back, his hands out in a placating gesture. "We don't have time for games. I'll give you the shortened version of what you need to know, and then you decide."

I kept my blade firmly gripped and made sure that it drifted between me and him.

"Fair enough. Spit it out, then."

"Everything you've heard about me is a lie. I do not eat little children for breakfast, nor do I enjoy raping and pillaging. The other Knights despise me because I refuse to be part of the Conclave. My father and all the ancestors before him have kept the rest of Arkor at bay by using the propaganda of fear. I'd also rather be feared so that the other Knights will leave me and my people alone. I protect what I cherish, just as you would Princess."

I narrowed my eyes at him, and my next words were an accusation. "Is that so? Then tell me why I saw a string of impaled skeletons strung farther than the eye could see a few summers ago when traveling with my father to the borders of your realm?" *See if you can explain your way out of this one.*

Drake looked at me sadly. "Before one of my subjects dies, they choose what will be done with their body. Some donate their body for anatomical research. Others choose to donate their body for the defense of the Kingdom. They can die satisfied knowing that their skeletons will be used as part of the Wall of Fear to deter outsiders. Those skeletons are of people who have died of natural causes and illnesses, not people whom I have had killed, Princess."

Damn him. He sounded so reasonable that I wanted to tear his eyes out. So instead I said this: "What do you have to say for yourself about this…That anyone who ventures into your Kingdom is never heard from again? If you're so benevolent, explain *that*."

Again the Knight gave me a sad look, as if he wished none of this were necessary. "It is true that I must keep my Kingdom safe, and that means secrecy. Those who enter my lands are compelled to stay. For a time they are watched and forced, but eventually I let them choose. Those who still want to leave are given a potion of forgetfulness so that they can't reveal anything. The others stay as my subjects by their own free will."

He stepped forward boldly, his own life forgotten as he reached out to rest two hands on my shoulders.

My hand clenched around the hilt of my sword, but I didn't bring it up to strike him. Instead I saw the desperation in his eyes.

The desperation of needing to be believed. I felt his hands warm my skin through the fabric of my tunic.

"I would debate the matter to your satisfaction if I could, Princess, but time is not on our side. Lady Agwen has apparently decided that you being banished to my Kingdom as a bride-to-be is too good for you. She's mustered an army, and she means to see you dead."

So, the mother of the Red Knight really does have that much hatred toward me. Could I blame her? I'd killed her son. Yet the fierce, stubborn voice of my brother broke into my mind. *No, Naji. No bride deserves to be slapped and beaten in her wedding bed for the groom's enjoyment. What you did when you reached out and took the knife wasn't wrong. It was instinct. You were protecting yourself.*

Tears gathered at my eyes, but I swiped at them before they could fall down my cheeks.

"Naji, what do you want to do? I'll follow your lead," Bronwyn said.

To my shock I said these words: "Leave us, please."

Bronwyn looked like she hadn't heard me right.

"Please. It's okay. Wait for me in the tent."

Reluctantly my friend finally listened, and then it was just me and the handsome Black Knight, face to face with what seemed an electrified chemistry stirring between us.

"Why are you doing this? You would fight an entire army to protect me?"

Drake looked at me with caring eyes which were now storm grey under the cloud-obscured sky. "She was a servant in the Red Knight's household. The spy I told you about. She'd seen him hurt many other women. She'd sometimes been a victim herself. What you did took great courage."

He carefully wrapped his arms around me, and I felt his chin rest on top of my head. I felt encased. His warmth surrounded me, even through his body armor.

"I've admired you and wanted to help you ever since that night, Naji. When my spies told me of your fate, I promised myself that as soon as you got close enough to my Kingdom, as soon as I had the power and resources to help you, I would." He tilted my face upward and looked at me.

I couldn't believe I was doing this, but I did it. My hands clasped the sides of his face, bringing it down to mine for a slow kiss, probationary at first. Then the kiss become a full blown lips to lips, mouth on mouth connection. I finally broke away, my heart hammering in my chest as I looked up at him.

"That's how we say 'I believe you' in the White Kingdom," I told him with a wry look. He stared back at me carefully as if unsure that this was what I wanted.

"Princess Najika, I swear to be your Champion. To protect you and to guard you with my life. I swear this, also; I will not be like the other Knights you have known. I know you have no special reason to trust me. The other Knights who betrayed you and wanted to condemn you to death were no less handsome than me. They were no less skilled with a blade or powerful. But being a Knight isn't about ornate armor, weapons of power, or flowery speech. For me it's about something else. It's about being a protector."

Drake looked into my eyes and said those words with an earnest face that had me recalling a fond memory. The son of a nobleman telling me that he wanted me to be his girl as we sat in the branches of the peach tree in the royal gardens, our faces covered in fruit juices. Right now was a moment of total vulnerability, and I found it working its appalling magic on me.

"That's certainly…more than anyone else has ever promised me," I said, my heart pounding. "Words are cheap, though, wouldn't you say?" I gave him a wicked grin. "I assume you have a battle plan?"

As if my approval had turned him from a toad into a prince, the Black Knight became the inscrutable man I'd first seen on the shore of the bathing pool. Drake nodded. "I believe so, Princess. If you'll join me, then we must speak with the trolls. Lady Agwen's army has moved to block Greyrock Pass, and she knows there is no other way back into my Kingdom…not without a detour that would take us ten days out of our way."

His eyes turned to steel. "I'd rather nip this nightmare in the bud. I don't think Lady Agwen will defer her vengeance. If we don't strike her a blow now, she'll keep adding to her forces and invade my Kingdom."

The thought of the woman who'd raised the Red Knight no longer gave me fear. It made me angry. I wondered how many other victims she'd helped her son abuse and forced to keep quiet about it. A lethal smile spread over my face.

"We can't have that, can we? I guess we'll have to kill the bitch."

My vulgar language took the Black Knight by surprise. "Those are not the words of a Lady," he said with a frown.

I shrugged. "I thought you liked 'feisty' women?" I turned my back on him and prepared to gather up the rest of my gear. Apparently I was about to fight in my first battle.

Chapter 6

Battles were not the stuff of romance I thought they were. I wasn't prepared for the carnage that followed. I wasn't ready for the terrifying, heart-rending images that my eyes could never un-see.

Lady Agwen's standard was a red lion and stag intertwined on a field of gold. Her battle standard flapped in the breeze as her knights took up their formations. Their steeds were armored, the knights' lances sharpened to fine points as the horn blew and the ranks surged into motion.

I sat beside Drake, who looked like a creature out of nightmare in his black body armor and horned helm. The trolls had formed up like ranks of wheat on either side of us, tightly packed and swaying, chanting in their strange, harsh-sounding tongue.

"What are they doing?"

"Gathering up their courage just like us," he replied. Bronwyn stood with the archers well behind the front lines. She was a doughty girl, but her farming father had never trained her to fight from horseback as I had been.

"I really hope this works," I said, worry skittering up and down my arms. My stomach clenched. I wanted to vomit.

"The knights of the Red Kingdom may be valiant, but they've never fought trolls," the Black Knight replied.

The time for talk was done, and the waves of armored death were nearly on us. The lances swung level, ready to skewer us all as the drumbeat of hooves filled my ears. The knee-high grass could hide much, though, and right now they hid giant shields several inches thick. At the call of the trolls' battle horn suddenly there was a desperate heaving of ropes and trolls in a frenzy at the base of each shield struggled to keep them from sliding from their appointed places.

All along the battle line the shields rose up, each twice the height of a man, and in the next instant the wave of Agwen's knights slammed into that obstacle with a terrible force. I heard the sounds of shrieking men, shouting trolls, and terrified horses. Battle was joined, and for a moment I watched with my hands twitching on the hilt of my sword, eager to become wrapped up in the chaos.

Some of the horses managed to punch through with sheer force, but most of the shield wall held. The few knights who did plunge through were quickly overwhelmed by trolls swinging clubs as long as saplings. They would swing with a resounding THWACK, crunching bone and denting armor as the knights desperately tried to hack their way forward. But each time the trolls were able to plug up the gap. The knights of the Red Kingdom milled about uncertainly with the shield wall holding firm when Drake raised his hand and threw it down in a vicious motion, giving the signal 'Let the arrows fly!'

I imagined Bronwyn and the other trolls unleashing a thousand shafts into the air, and then I saw them, a cloud of pointy killers which blotted out part of the sky and arced towards the enemy. The first wave of arrows pelted the knights and horses, but their armor seemed to deflect most of them. I shot Drake a puzzled look.

"That didn't seem to faze them," I said.

"Just watch."

I looked back and realized that there was a new kind of screaming coming from the mass of knights. This was a different flavor of scream from the one that came with the crunch of bone. Some of the knights' armor was smoking, the metal literally melting as they writhed and pitched off their horses.

"Acid. The most aggressive kind," the Black Knight told me with grim finality.

That was when the floodgates opened. With the knights of the Red Kingdom in disarray and with all of Lady Agwen's forces committed to the battle, it was time for a push of our own.

"Are you ready, Princess?"

I drew my weapon, hoping that was answer enough.

The shield wall tumbled down as the trolls war-whooped with their hair-raising, inhuman cry of rage. The trolls were not well armored. In fact they wore nothing but the many layers of cloth wrappings they seemed so fond of. But seeing them move was like watching acrobats, and their giant clubs were swung with the ease I might swing a twig—except each one was nearly as thick as a tree trunk.

Drake had one squad of trusted knights who'd accompanied him on this expedition outside of his own Kingdom. They flanked us, giving me a false sense of safety as we thundered onto the battlefield. It wasn't long before I met my first enemy knight. He was older, and he didn't look especially regretful as his sword leapt to tear out my throat. I ducked underneath the attack, parried a second blow, and then slashed at his foot, drawing a bright ribbon of blood as he screamed and lunged over to stab me through.

I brought my shield up, deflecting the strike only to have him use his own shield as a weapon. He bashed it against my helm, disorienting me. I dropped my shield as he repositioned the blade for another thrust—one I didn't have a prayer of avoiding.

His eyes went wide as Drake's great-sword created a line where his shoulder blade had been.

No sword could cut through armor like that except an enchanted weapon. Something only a Knight would have. *It's an artifact of power, you idiot.* I should've known. Drake handed me his spare shield and told me sternly. "Stay close, Princess. I want this to be your *first* battle, not your last."

He waded ahead, dealing death as he went. Crimson knights fell in his wake, and I followed him. My goal for the day had rapidly changed from 'Find glory and slay the enemy' to 'Try not to die, Naji.'

I ducked under a brutal attack from another mounted knight, swept my own blade out instinctually. My blow came before he could react, glancing off of his helm. The force behind my blow sent him reeling, and before he could recover I thrust between the joints of the plates which protected his groin. With a cry of pain he felt my blade sink in, draining his life blood as I drew it back out. I cantered my horse forward.

He hadn't been the first man I'd ever killed, but it was the first time I'd ever killed a man with that kind of premeditation, knowing for a fact that it was me or him.

I focused on the present, discarding my guilt and taking in the carnage around me. It was horrific. This was not the glorious battle I'd envisioned. It was desperate life against life. It was men and trolls, some with their entrails pouring out of them as they lay lifeless. It was bellows of rage and pain. A troll next to me died, his neck almost severed. Blood spattered my face, covered the visor of my helm. I had to yank the thing off and wipe at my face just to be able to see, and that's when I felt an arrow punch into my shoulder, tearing into the body armor.

My left arm felt a spasm of pain and I turned, confused. Lady Agwen's forces hadn't had any archers. So why...

That's when I realized that on the ridge overlooking the battlefield a tall, green standard with a charging unicorn flapped in the breeze.

It was the Green Knight's standard, and his archers, rows upon rows of them, were starting to unleash volleys of death into both the knights of the Red Kingdom and our own forces indiscriminately.

Beside him a woman rode on a tall chestnut horse. She wore a crown, its centerpiece fixed with a diamond. Even without being close enough to see the detail, I *knew*. It was her. Lady Agwen. Had she willingly sacrificed her entire army to lure us into a trap? That's the only thing that made sense, and it also meant that the Green Knight had formed an unusual alliance with her.

We were doomed.

I looked around frantically, and Drake was suddenly there by my side. "Are you hurt?" He grappled at my shoulder, eyeing the depth of the penetration. With a tug he tore the shaft free and tossed it aside.

"It barely pierced the skin. You were lucky. Now come. We must go." He gestured for me to follow, but I stubbornly sheathed my sword and reached for my bow. I had been an expert markswoman when Father trained me. The range was extreme, but Lady Agwen was not beyond bowshot. I prepared to nock an arrow when Drake grabbed me roughly by the arm.

"Najika, listen to me. Don't be a fool. I care for you." Those words *care for you* hit me like a blow. The insanity of those words coming from a man who had gore splattered over half of his torso almost made me smirk, but instead I nodded and let him guide me in retreat.

"So much for your brilliant plan, Sir Knight," I said as we cantered free of the carnage. The trolls were regrouping at the edge of the forest which faced the ridge, but just when I thought we might have a chance of turning this thing around a blood curdling yell came from the shadows of those same trees. Men-at-arms in chainmail armed with spears rushed into the open, working in a planned formation as they slammed into the surprised trolls. It was like watching clay pigeons smashed by a sling's stone then shatter into a million pieces. The trolls broke ranks and fled, except there was nowhere to flee *to*.

The rest of the trolls near the center of the battlefield had frantically repositioned the shield wall to give them a break from the showers of arrows which the Green Knight's archers were flinging at them one after another, but it was only a matter of time before what was left of our army felt the squeeze of the Green Knight's intended sandwich. The Green Knight's mounted knights were ready to outflank us on either side of the ridge, and his spear-bristling soldiers advanced at a deliberate pace from the opposite direction.

"I didn't want to have to do this, Princess." He handed me a conch. "Please do the honors and blow, hard as you can." The shell seemed to gleam as I put it uncertainly to my lips. I blew with all my strength, the air whooshing from my lungs.

It made a satisfying, low rumble and then something in the air seemed to shift.

"You know, Princess, although the Knights of Arkor don't like to admit it, there are items of magical worth besides their precious 'artifacts of power.'" Drake turned to me, grim humor in his eyes. "Be prepared to flee for your life."

"I thought that's what we were doing."

"We were, but in a moment we'll actually have a prayer of escaping," Drake said, and in the distance what began as a rumble had begun to sound like a deep, deep thunder-crack under the earth.

I gaped. My jaw went slack and I whispered a few un-ladylike words as three towering monstrosities came into view.

"Befriending the trolls was never an accident, Princess. We both see the other Knights of Arkor as what they are—treacherous backstabbers always looking for power. There was once a time when the only semi-sentient beings in Arkor were an ancient breed of giant trolls who roamed the land unchallenged. The magical Horn of Calling I gave you is old enough and blessed with a magic that opens a rift in time itself to call them to the present."

I tried to stop gaping. "They look pissed."

"They are. Being pulled out of your own time period will do that. It's one reason I hate to invoke the horn. No creature should be ripped so violently from their home. They will look for whatever they can to smash. To destroy things, in their grief."

I noticed exactly that as the first of the lumbering giant trolls began to run along the ridge where the Green Knight's archers had been lined up in such neat formation. That formation now crumbled in a flurry of screams, thrown hands, and discarded bows as each man ran for his life. I could see what I thought might be the Green Knight's figure, gesturing rapidly and trying to rally his archers to throw a deadly volley at the rampaging troll.

The other two giant trolls crashed through the center of the battlefield, sending our own forces retreating headlong in all directions. A sizeable chunk of our army ran directly for the forest. The bristling formation of soldiers saw our trolls coming their way, and at first I imagined they probably felt elation. But when the giant trolls swerved to follow, each step pounding the ground like an earthquake, the line of spearmen wavered. A few more heartbeats and then they broke ranks altogether, hoping to reach the relative safety of the trees before their human-sized troll counterparts.

Chaos was unfolding all around us, and with it a hope flared in my chest.

I looked up at the ridge and saw the figure of Lady Agwen. She still sat astride her horse, her bearing stiff and proud. She was so close, and now that the Green Knight's forces were melting away in panic...A thought blossomed from a kernel to a conviction, and I reached for my sword, ready to spur my horse to a gallop.

A hand gently folded around my wrist.

"Princess, this is our opportunity. We go now, while we can."

I turned back to him, my eyes pleading. "Come with me. We can kill her in the confusion." I understood this sudden need in my heart, to see this woman dead. The more I thought of what her son had done to me, done to others, the more she became the surrogate for everything I hated. For what had taken my innocence.

"Killing her isn't going to take away the pain, Naji." He used my familiar name, and his eyes were stern at the edges but somehow soft at the center.

"I'm sorry, but this is something I have to do. If she had just told the truth, Father wouldn't have disowned me. My life wouldn't have been completely ruined. I need to finish this."

Drake glanced up at the giant troll up on the ridge. He had uprooted several trees and was swinging them back and forth, using the archers as targets. The mounted knights who tried to charge the beast did no better. One mighty swing swept them away like powder, and the troll's roars of grief filled the air. I suddenly wondered if the thing had a concept of family. If it had a father, mother, wife, or children left behind when the Horn of Calling ripped it from its own time and brought it to ours.

I shook my head clear of the thought, refocusing my mind on the woman I needed to kill.

I urged my horse forward and Drake kept up. He put his hand on my reins, bringing me up short as I glared at him, my voice filled with rage.

"I've made my choice, Drake. Join me or don't, but don't try to stop me!" He looked at me carefully, as if I was as fragile as a clay figure, and he leaned over, his hand grasping the nape of my neck.

He put his forehead softly against mine, bringing our eyes so close. I saw the genuine ache in him, and he said the words slowly, as if trying to penetrate through many layers of rock. *Or in this case your thick skull, stupid girl.* My brother's voice echoed in my head as I felt Drake's lips softly brush against mine and then pull away.

"I understand. You hardly know me, and it's easier to grieve the life you've lost than start from scratch. But that's what I'm offering you, Princess, and if you go up that ridge I can't help you. There are over a thousand hostile knights and archers on that ridge and a rampaging troll taller than a castle wall. You may think you can do this, but let me tell you—you can't. And even if you could kill Lady Agwen, what would it change? Would it ease the gash in your heart?"

It can't, but maybe he can, said a little voice in my head. I looked up at him. This was *it*. I needed to decide, now or never. I turned back to the ridge and watched as Lady Agwen galloped clear of the bloodbath. It took me a moment to realize that there were tears streaming down my face. That the choking sobs torn from my chest were really *mine*.

I didn't try to go back. Not anymore. I took Drake's hand and used it as leverage to jump behind him on the saddle. My hands curved tightly around his chest.

"Hold on tight. We're getting out of here, Princess." I sniffed, blinking and smearing tears on the Black Knight's back as he swerved between obstacles, narrowly avoiding a dead horse which almost tripped up his mount and brought us all sprawling.

The sounds of dying and of battle receded behind us, and then we were free—just two people on a horse with a sea of waving grass to urge us on.

Chapter 7

"Any ideas?" I asked.

"Plenty. The problem is none of them are all that good," he replied.

Drake eyed the narrow bridge over the gaping chasm of Greyrock Pass. If two sea monsters had lain end to end, it still wouldn't have been as wide as the gap. Drake's people called it the Bridge of Sorrows because of the weepy fog that always hung over it like a funeral shroud.

"I'm assuming we can't just cut our way through?" I gave Drake a bold look, then glanced back at the knights guarding the bridge. They wore the Green Knight's unicorn crest on their breastplates, which meant they were in league with Lady Agwen. Why the Green Knight had decided to help her try to kill me I didn't exactly know, but the Green Knight was known as an opportunist. I was sure whatever it was, Agwen had made it worth his while. *They deserve each other.* The not-so-charitable part of me was already imagining ways to torture them. But seeing as I was the fugitive and they had two entire Kingdoms under their control, maybe I was getting ahead of myself.

"We could wait until nightfall," Drake mused, but the way he chewed on his bottom lip didn't look hopeful.

"We *could* fall over the edge, not seeing where we're going, and never be heard from again," I said. "When I asked about ideas, I meant ones where we *don't* die horribly."

Drake shot me a look. "When I first saw you naked and beautiful bathing in the waterfall pool, I didn't know you had such a mouth on you." My cheeks flushed and my mouth fell open, but I wasn't going to give the idiot the satisfaction of being speechless.

"Maybe if you'd let me kill Lady Agwen in the first place we wouldn't be in this mess!" The sudden flare of anger surprised me. It had been a few hours since we'd been separated from Drake's surviving knights in the confusion of the battle. The bridge was the quickest way to cross over into the Black Kingdom and safety, but the question was 'how?'.

"For all I know Bronwyn might be dead. What if she didn't make it out?" My thoughts sobered as I worried about the only friend I had in the world besides my supposed husband-to-be. My emotions skittered like stones in a rock slide. She was my best friend and I'd abandoned her back there. I had let the Black Knight rescue me when I should have stayed to fight.

"If you'd stayed and fought, then gotten yourself killed trying to find Bronwyn while giant trolls rampaged in all directions, how do you think she would have felt?" Drake said. I hadn't realized I'd verbalized my last thought. My face crumbled, and for a moment I felt sick. I wanted to throw up.

"Bronwyn's best chance of escaping would have been to slip away unobtrusively, and from what I can tell she's a pretty resourceful girl. Like someone else I know. I wouldn't write her off just yet."

The warmth crinkling at the edge of Drake's eyes made my breath hitch. Suddenly I was acting with blind instinct. We were hidden inside a cluster of aspen trees as if nature had made a tiny room just for us. Abruptly I leaned over, my lips finding his. For an instant I felt him stiffen, startled as if a lightning bolt had whipped its way through every vein in his body. Then Drake melted into the kiss, his hands fisting in my hair as his mouth responded voraciously to mine. His smell enveloped me, making me forget that I was a runaway prisoner banished from my own Kingdom. It was a sweet taste of forgetfulness that burrowed into my head.

"Princess." Somehow our mouths had finally disengaged. Drake was looking at me carefully, as if I were a breakable thing. Which I wasn't. For some reason it both enflamed and annoyed me, the soft way he looked at me.

My gaze hardened, and I tried to forget my lapse of reason. *What in the sweet mercies were you thinking, Naji? You hardly know this man.* Yet he'd saved my life. If a person's actions were a good shortcut to knowing someone, then I already knew Drake on a level I couldn't claim for most people.

"I knew it," he said.

"Knew what?" I folded my arms across my chest, my stare cooling.

"That kissing you again would be sublime," he said simply. It was hard to know how to respond to that. But he seemed able to turn it off, sensing the panic in my face the longer we stood within bowshot of who knew how many knights who had orders to kill or capture me.

"I want more of those kisses…and if I can get you to the Black Kingdom where I rule, I plan to demand them," he said, a teasing humor in his voice. His eyes were already clouding over in thought, however, and his mind seemed to be sifting through one idea after the next.

We stood in silence, the occasional chittering squirrel in the tree branches giving us unhelpful advice. I took stock of what we had. I still had my sword, a long knife, the bow and iron-tipped arrows in my quiver. Drake had his great-sword and not much else, but as a new idea sparked in my head, I thought what we had just might be enough.

"Sometimes you're right, Drake. The direct method doesn't always pan out. If I'd gone after Lady Agwen I probably would have gotten myself killed," I admitted ruefully. His eyes snapped up to meet mine, surprised at my confession.

"But now I need *you* to trust *me*." I began to strip out of my armor.

"Najika, what are you doing?"

My eyes arched, daring him to ask me again. "Trust," was all I muttered. Soon I was in just my tunic and leggings. I rolled my shoulders, feeling the stiffness in them finally loosen now that I was out of the restrictive hug of the armor. I picked up my bow and secured the quiver of arrows.

"You want to protect me?" I asked.

Drake nodded slowly, trying to determine where this was going, and his hesitation told me he didn't expect to like the destination.

"Good, because I'm about to give you the chance. I want you to circle around. I'm going to provide a distraction. You're going to attack from behind."

Drake put his hands on my shoulders and shook me to add emphasis to his words. "We don't know how many there are, Naji. We've seen at least ten men lounging on this side of the bridge. For all we know, there could be more."

I pulled free of his grip, ran out into the open, nocked an arrow, and fired.

The projectile spun in a perfect dovetail, piercing the hide of the horse underneath one of the patrolling knights. In the fog I didn't have a prayer of hitting an exposed gap in a knight's armor, but a horse made a decent target. The poor beast reared with a loud shriek, sending its rider slipping backward. As the horse spun and raged, the knight was thrown clear and the rest of the knights responded. They came at me, their armor clanking. Two of the onrushing knights were mounted, and my arrows whispered harmlessly through the fog, unable to snag those fast-moving targets. Not that it mattered. I turned and fled, angling towards the denser but not too dense part of the forest. There were small clearings here and there where avalanches or rock slides had cleared out some of the forest's old growth. I ran, easily able to outpace the laboring knights and even the two mounted knights, whose horses had to carefully pick a path through maples and aspens.

I led them ever deeper into the woods but made sure the ones at the head of the pursuit didn't lose sight of me. No easy task as the fog caressed my arms and face.

Come on, Drake. See the opportunity and take it. From a logical standpoint my plan could work, but the odds against us would have had Drake trying to convince me out of it. Was the plan insane on some level? Maybe. But it was a plan, and in theory it would work.

Perhaps all those strategy lessons with my father's war historian had rubbed off on me. Who knew?

"Halt! Surrender or we will be forced to harm you!" Those cries were coming from the two mounted knights. Finally I slowed down, whirling around as I stopped in a small clearing. In the middle of running for my life all I had managed were a few backward glances, and it had seemed like at least 15 knights were on my trail. Now there were...three. The two mounted knights flanked me and then began to circle as the third knight came up on foot, his helmed face hidden from view.

"Princess Najika, surrender and you will be quietly taken into the care of our lord and master, the Green Knight."

"The same lord and master who has treacherously allied with the woman trying to kill me? You must think I'm as dumb as your mother," I retorted. I drew my sword with a flourish. In the fog it looked dull and less impressive than I'd hoped. "If you want your manhood handed to you at the edge of a blade, I suggest you come forward." My impudence was having the right effect. The knight on foot angrily drew his own sword and muttered an oath about making me suffer under his attentions in the dungeons for that remark. I prepared for the clash of swords even as the mounted knights looked ready to rush in and take me from behind, but then a shadow unexpectedly parted the mists. A black-armored shadow overlaying pure muscle and desperate rage.

Drake had taken his sweet time, but he'd made his appearance when it counted.

The knight rushing towards me barely had time to register the black-helmed knight as a sword as long as my torso neatly sliced through his armor as if it were made of ice instead of metal. The armor sheared in half, the knight's body along with it, and what strode over the remains was a tall, forbidding figure holding a great sword, the sword hilt sporting a fearsome dragon whose ruby eyes blazed even through the fog.

I turned back, all too aware of the mounted knights shifting atop their warhorses, sizing up Drake and preparing to run him down.

Each of the knights wearing the Green Knight's crest spurred their beasts forward, aiming to hit Drake in a one-two succession so that even if he somehow recovered from the first attack, the second attacker could smite him from above with his weaknesses laid bare. The knights flung their mounts into the charge. The first knight had his lance leveled and the second knight drew his sword, preparing to finish off Drake after his companion landed the first disorienting blow.

They had forgotten about the little, dainty princess. Poor harmless, helpless me. Despite the fact that most princesses received battle training, some knights had a hard time remembering that even physically weaker foes had brains and knew how to use them.

Like a bucket brigade trying to snuff out a blazing fire, arrows flew from my quiver, each nocked at my bow before flying in a deadly zing, one after the next. I let the smooth motion settle in my limbs, my arm flinging back, releasing, hand gripping the next shaft to fling its iron-tipped 'Hi there!' of death. My arm burned as I let those arrows fly, not at the knights, but at the much easier targets of their mounts. One of my arrows dug into the first horse's mane and it jerked, stumbling as the pain lanced through its concentration. Though I felt sorry for the animal, I didn't have the luxury of hesitation. Its master was about to kill a man, a man I liked…maybe more than liked. A man who had saved my life, and now I was returning the favor.

I sent another flurry of arrows at the knights, and by the time the knight with the lance reached Drake my damage had been done. The first knight's horse had badly altered its original course. Although the knight tried to reposition, his lance shot harmlessly wide as Drake easily sidestepped the puncturing blow.

Now it was the Black Knight's turn. I watched as Drake's sword cut in a vicious arc, spraying blood and other things best left unmentioned. The knight's shoulders shifted as he looked down, unable to believe the work that Drake's enchanted great-sword had done. The body twitched in two pieces as it bloodied the ground with a rasping gurgle.

The second knight hesitated, but his trajectory was already taking him into Drake's path. The knight's sword came down, bashing Drake's helm. The hit disoriented Drake, and I saw him stumble, leaving an opening for the knight to finish him with a killing thrust. My arrows were still hissing through the fog, though, and one of them glanced off of the enemy knight's helm like an irritation. It distracted him for only a pair of heartbeats, but that was enough.

Drake had dropped his great-sword, yet being unarmed didn't seem to discourage him. With a roar that would have made most predators envious, Drake grabbed the enemy knight by the wrist, hauling him from the saddle. I gaped as Drake threw the man as if he weighed no more than a sack of feathers.

I admired the knight's ability to get up from that still intact, and he lunged at Drake with a deadly thrust. Drake batted the blade aside almost contemptuously, and then he traded the knight blow for blow, his armored fists raining punishment. The knight dropped his sword, trying to shield himself from the blows and return a few of his own. The Black Knight was relentless though, and he picked up his opponent's fallen sword, thrusting for the exposed gap between the breastplate and helm. The green-armored knight stiffened, his body shuddering as a strangled cry tore through the forest. With brutal efficiency Drake rammed the blade the rest of the way through. As the man dropped, Drake dropped on his knees beside him, his breathing ragged.

As I ran up to him I could see the hammering exhaustion of a heart ready to burst. I knelt beside him as he took off his helm. I looked into his sweat-slick face, and his eyes settled on mine with a fury that made me flinch.

"If you ever, *ever* do that again I'm going to kiss the lips off of you and spank you at the same time," he said between raspy breaths.

I honored him with a cross look of my own. "It worked, didn't it?"

"Worked?" he said between pants. "Worked!?" he cried. "Yes, I was able to sneak up and attack from behind, taking them out one by one in the confusion and the fog, and it was only possible because they were all so focused on you." He managed to get his feet under him, and his arms drew me into a bone-rattling hug, his hand cupping the back of my head. "That your insane plan 'worked' doesn't excuse you of your sins, though. What if I hadn't been quick enough? What if they hadn't been so single-minded in their pursuit?"

"Yet I knew that they *would* be," I replied. I could have explained to Drake that the Green Knight was known for motivating his soldiers with bounty rewards, that I had been fairly certain that the knights chasing me were seeing chests of gold in the backs of their heads as I ran. But that would have taken all the fun out of tormenting him.

"You just knew?" he echoed with disbelief. It was the kind of disbelief when you couldn't believe someone could be so amazingly crazy or stupid.

"Do you still want to marry me?" I said, smiling as if this were just an ordinary day. "Because if so, I suggest less whining and more moving. We don't know if there might be a few stragglers. I'm guessing if we circle back we can find a gap in the patrol and sneak our way over the bridge, assuming we didn't kill everyone."

"We?" he asked. Blood and gore covered every inch of his armor like a madman's mural.

"I did help," I protested. "I was the brains. You were the muscle. Deal with it." I hadn't meant to be so harsh, but constantly being on the run had stretched my humanity to a breaking point, and after surviving the battle at Drake's side whatever shyness I'd felt toward him had vanished.

He shook his head, muttering curses as we moved to let the forest enfold us in deeper shadow. It took the rest of the afternoon, but we finally maneuvered back to the bridge and kept watch long enough to determine that we'd destroyed the force guarding it. Before darkness fell we had crossed the bridge. I was entering the Kingdom no one had ever told me about as a child, the Kingdom I first knew existed only by listening to hushed whispers. The Black Kingdom.

Chapter 8

The Black Kingdom, Eleven Months Later…

Bronwyn smiled at me. She did that often now, and it wasn't the 'Poor, breakable friend, I hope she's okay' smile that Bronwyn had used for the first few months we were in the Black Knight's Kingdom. It was a smile just happy for me, no undercurrents of worry.

And that made me even happier as I hummed and readjusted my sword belt. I had a training sword tightened at my waist. Today was sparring day. At my request Drake was teaching me new sword fighting tricks. By all accounts I was a quick learner. I would soon be besting him.

"What do you think? Will the distraction help?" I twirled like a total girl, the cream-colored tunic cut low, revealing bare shoulders and tantalizing cleavage.

"Najika! I'm shocked. Really. Would a princess like you stoop so low that you'd use the lushness of the feminine form to distract your opponent? That hardly seems fair!" Bronwyn cried.

"A win is a win, sister, and I'll take it however I can, thank you very much."

Just then Drake strode in, his sparring tunic hugging his muscular shoulders nice and tightly. We both melted into giggles as his eyes widened at the shirt I wore.

"Do you plan to fight in that?" he said, mystified.

Bronwyn mouthed goodbye and slipped out the back. She had a new horse to train, which always made her giddy. Meanwhile I put my hands behind my back, thrusting out my breasts and torturing Drake just because I could.

"Why? Is that going to be a problem for you?"

"It is if you want to spar today. I might simply surrender before you strike the first blow," he replied, rushing forward and taking me in his arms. I grinned as he kissed me, his hands roving down my back and cupping a certain curvaceous area.

When he drew back, though, his gaze had grown serious. Too serious. My eyes narrowed.

"What? Is something wrong?" We'd been cautiously treating one another as each other's betrothed for more than six months, but it had all remained unofficial. There was a time when I hadn't known where I'd end up, when I'd only accepted the Black Knight's hospitality until I could figure out where I wanted to go next.

"Yes, something is very wrong. Princess Najika, daughter of the White Kingdom, I have a very important question for you."

My heart stilled. Drake had purposefully not pressured me these past several months. He'd been patient with me. He'd won me over just because of who he was as a person, not because of his power, influence, or anything else. I'd learned that the myth of the evil Black Knight was just that, a myth.

My hand went to my face, covering my gaping mouth as he drew out a ring. It was studded with gems—emeralds, rubies, amethysts, sapphires—and a sparkling diamond was now giving me its knowing wink.

No, Naji. He didn't. He...no, he can't be asking this. I refused to cry. It was absolutely not an option.

"The one thing I can see wrong in the world right now is that you are not my wife. So I have to ask the most beautiful, kind, brave, and amazing woman I know one simple question: Will you marry me?"

I didn't cry. Tears don't count until they drip off the bottoms of your cheekbones. Everyone knows that. He kissed me then, and I realized that I was going to be okay. I was no longer the Princess of the White Kingdom.

I would be the Queen of the Black Kingdom. It was us against the world, and the dreams I'd been having included Drake in my life, for better or for worse. For as long as forever might last.

End of Part One

####

Chapter 9

"Naji, you're trembling."

Weddings weren't exactly my cup of chicken broth. At least not since the night I'd killed my first husband. Nerves weren't the only thing haunting me as we stood by the finely carved altar in the ancient grove. Ever bigger circles of the Black Knight's guests watched us from all sides and every angle. Among them stood one ambassador sent from each Kingdom, here to confirm the 'good will' and new relationship between the Black Kingdom and the Kingdoms of all the other colors. Just then I had thoughts of my father, the Knight and lord ruler of the White Kingdom, and a shiver turned my spine into one long icicle.

At about the same time a wave of nausea churned my insides. What little breakfast I'd dared to eat now offered to make a return appearance, and it took every scrap of strength to force it back down.

Drake was doing this all for me, and I hated it. I hated that he was willing to risk his whole Kingdom to marry me. The baggage I'd brought to our relationship was the size of a mound of ogre dung and just as difficult to ignore.

Do you really deserve this, Naji...after what you've done? I'd killed the Red Knight and left the Blue Knight in a poison-induced coma. Somehow I thought my chances for winning the princess-of-the-year contest had slipped through my fingertips. The same fingertips that seemed so capable of murder.

"Take my hands." Drake's hands reached out, enfolding mine. He and I both knew that these were not the wedding day jitters of an ordinary woman marrying an ordinary man. The memory of my first wedding to the Red Knight bled into my thoughts like a reopened wound. I remembered the aftermath of that first wedding ceremony. The Red Knight's fists on my body the moment we entered the bedchamber. The sadistic triumph in his eyes each time he landed a blow or a slap calculated not to leave any obvious mark...

My muscles tensed like an animal needing to run. Somewhere. Anywhere. Just away from the here and now. The similarities didn't help. All of the men and ladies dressed in their finest, looking expectantly at me. The officiating monk in his ivory-fringed shawl, his tonsured head nodding as he handed us the rings and began the vows. The polite, veiled looks barely concealing disdain or outright hate that came from the ambassadors from across all the Kingdoms of Arkor.

"Do you, Princess Najika of the White Kingdom, renounce your status and swear your undying love and devotion to this man, Sir Drake, Knight and overlord of the Black Kingdom?"

I forced myself to look into Drake's eyes and see nothing else. I found steadiness there and pretended the rest of the world didn't exist.

"I do."

"Do you, Sir Drake, promise to take Princess Najika and place her on the throne beside you as your Queen, to rule as your equal in all things and to adjudicate in matters of justice?"

My chest swelled. Now this part was *quite different* than my first wedding. In all the Kingdoms of Arkor, among the Knights of all the other colors, a Queen might have powers and privileges, but she never shared in her husband's status. Not really.

But the Black Kingdom was not the rest of Arkor. I looked into Drake's storm-grey eyes, lit up with possibility at the very mention of me as Queen, and it melted my heart. My breathing calmed as we finished the vows together, our fingers entwined through the whole ordeal. The tonsured monk finished his various head bobs and mutterings, none too soon for my liking, and finally...*finally* we were allowed to exit down an aisle lined with brightly painted marker stones.

As the trees of the forest draped their arms around us, my nerves finally released their death grip on my brain and body. I walked quietly in my glossy black gown, mesmerized by the rubies studded around my belt which winked here and there under the dappled moonlight.

"A tent has been prepared for you," the chamberlain was saying. I saw it some ways off, fringed with tapestries, all puffed up in self-importance. Garlands of flowers heaped as high as my hips surrounded it like a moat. Drake's younger brothers, Ecthor and Fraey, gave their elder sibling a sly wink and a smile.

Other important people crowded around, solemnly congratulating us at the entrance to the tent before joining us inside.

My cheeks reddened as I saw the sumptuously laid bed sheets, probably made with fabric softer than a baby's bottom. I looked at the chamberlain and then back at my new husband. Then new flames leapt to my face as my mother-in-law, Lady Vaela, entered with her usual elegance.

"It is tradition, Naji, for the Promisekeeper to bless the marriage bed," Lady Vaela said, trying to soothe my obvious displeasure. Monks didn't deserve to have such a lofty title as 'Promisekeeper,' but I let it pass. I'd strangle the little imp and shave what hair he had left when this was all over. I also gave my mother-in-law a look which promised slow, painful torture before death.

She returned me a placid smile before politely watching the monk say his blessings.

"…And so we pray that an heir is conceived this night, assuring the future of this Kingdom and its people…" I blotted out everything after that. By this time I was seeing red. Why was it that the very man who probably knew the *least* about the act of conceiving had the sacred responsibility of blathering on about it?

After what seemed forever and a day, the monk graced us with his departure and the guests filed out, one after another, until it was just Lady Vaela, my new husband, and me. My mother-in-law looked at me calmly before giving her son a pointed look.

"May I speak with your bride alone for a few moments?" The words might have been phrased as a question, but the tone was iron. Drake was about to wade into battle for me despite it all, and I loved him for it, but I could fight my own battles.

"That will be all right, Drake. Really. A private blessing from your mother can do no harm, can it?"

Drake heard the strain in my pathetic attempt to sound natural, but he quietly bowed and left. Sometimes I regretted ever being born a princess. Why couldn't I have been born a normal girl, met a normal boy, and led a normal life without the impossible pressures of the world around me? When I'd been condemned for killing the Red Knight, I think part of me had been glad to finally have relief from the royal stage. Now I'd escaped the fire only to land promptly in the pit.

I turned to my mother-in-law. She was shorter than me, but you'd never know it from the way she carried herself. It was disgusting how unflappable she could be. She had blue eyes that somehow always came across as calm instead of icy, even when she was *furious*. Still, in the past eleven months and counting she'd made it clear that she didn't trust me, that she thought I'd probably committed the crime I'd been accused of...and that if I ever did anything to cause her son hurt or pain, she would make sure that I would suffer for it.

So, yes—I guess you could've called her a typical mother-in-law.

Lady Vaela pursed her lips. Was that a flicker of hesitation in her eyes? I gave her a confused look. I had expected a nasty warning. Certainly not this.

"If your goal is to kill me with anticipation, it's working," I said.

Vaela's pained expression only deepened my puzzlement. She made a shooing gesture with her hand. "Let's get this over with. I need you to take your clothes off. The spell won't work otherwise."

I made sure that my heart was still beating and that the words coming out of my mother-in-law's mouth were in a language I understood.

"I'm sorry. You'll have to repeat that."

Vaela's blond hair was piled atop her head like a royal crown. She sighed, a hand creasing her forehead before running up the curls as if an earthquake had embedded itself there.

"Has my son not told you that I am a sorceress?"

I nodded, blood thundering through my veins. My breathing quickened. What did this crazy, weird woman want?

"He told me that you have healing powers. You go out to the villages and sick people become well. But I am not sick and this...*this* is sick. I suggest you explain yourself."

Lady Vaela looked at me then, truly looked at me. I saw mistrust drain from her eyes for the first time. Instead there was this sympathy in her expression. It was like I was seeing a different person.

"It was not so long ago that I was standing where you are now, Najika. I can do other things...not just healing. Spells of protection. Warding. Passed down to me from my mother, and from hers before that. The point is, Najika..." Another heavy sigh. "If you do not want to become pregnant with child just yet, I can give you that protection. It is my experience that getting to know your husband and learning what it means to be a Queen is hard enough, even without a child on the way. It is my belief that you owe it to yourself to know who *you* are, and who you and my son are as two people joined—before a third enters the fray."

Lady Vaela's smooth face seamed with a wistful smile. She reached out a hand to catch a wisp of hair which had strayed from the simple ponytail I'd insisted on for the wedding.

"You...would do that for me?" I was pretty much speechless. That I could say this much was impressive.

My mother-in-law nodded. After a shudder and a sigh even more epic than the last, she finally spilled the beans.

"I know we got off to a rocky start, Najika. But I haven't been completely blind over the last year. I see the transformation in my son when he but *looks* at you. I also see the mettle you're made of. I've watched you train with my son and learn to fight as the seasons have turned. I may be stubborn, Najika. I may be protective of my son. But I'm not a senile old fool."

The suspicion in my eyes must have evaporated, because I found myself reaching out to clasp one of her frail hands in two of mine. I brought her hand to my lips, kissed the wrinkled skin with a tenderness I'd never felt towards her before, and then slowly let go.

"I do love your son," I said simply.

Lady Vaela nodded. "I know that now."

"Only took you, what, 340 days or so to figure that out?" I replied, trying to keep the acid in my voice at a teasing notch.

The crunch of footsteps abruptly sounded at the tent flap. "Can I have my bride back?" came Drake's impatient rumble.

"No!" came our replies in unison. It made me jump as a smile curled on my lips.

We waited until the crunching of boots faded, and then she gave me another impatient shooing gesture.

"Clothes. Off."

I couldn't believe I was doing this, but my gut telling me that someone I'd considered a mortal enemy now *wasn't*...well, that overrode embarrassment.

Chapter 10

The tent had become quite warm, at least in the bed we shared. The sounds of night creatures drifted through to us, but it was as if they were creating their symphony *just* for us. I couldn't claim this wasn't sentimental stupidity talking in my newly married, love-addled brain, but there it was.

I straddled him, and his eyes roved over my breasts.

"A bit distracted, aren't we?"

"What you call 'distracted' I call worshipping with my eyes. Have I ever told you how gorgeous the glow of a lantern's light looks on certain parts of your body?"

I had to stifle a giggle. These weren't exactly the undying romantic declarations I'd been taught to expect on my wedding night. Drake reached up, gently holding the breasts apparently so worthy of attention, and I watched his eyes slowly soak in the sight of my nakedness as if the most precious gem in the world had just slipped into view.

"Your body is every bit as beautiful as your heart Naji, and it's all mine," he said with a sly wink.

I bit my lip, giving him a sultry stare as I glanced down at what to me was just as beautiful. I saw the planes of his muscles fan out like a legendary map I wanted to read over and over again. I looked straight down, admiring the need in him.

"I'm yours, am I? And what of this? To whom does this belong?" I said with a teasing quirk of eyebrows.

In a flash we were what I might delicately call horizontal. I was gasping, Drake's body covering me like a blanket, moving in a pattern with mine. I hadn't known what to expect this night to be like…And this may not have been the graceful lovemaking the bards sang about in tales, the two of us fumbling and eager, tangled in the bed sheets. The awkwardness I'd first felt when Drake and I entered the tent wasn't crippling, though, and it didn't promise guilt after the fact. We knew each other, we'd committed to each other. Around Drake I felt *safe*. I trusted him and he trusted me, and it meant that ultimately nothing else could get in the way of that. Even the nerves I knew were hammering through both our hearts.

I guess I should have known that my life was going too well, too blissfully for fate to leave me alone. Something intruded on the perfect moment. A pale stripe of moonlight snuck into my eye, putting me on edge as a faint sound—not of nature—hissed between tent flaps which parted conveniently for an unseen breeze.

Except there was no breeze. There were two men covered head to toe in gray who had lifted the tent flap wide while a third partner raised his crossbow and fired. The bolt punched through the pillow where my head had just been. Luckily I'd tensed and rolled us clear of the sheets not a moment too soon.

We were still alive, but it didn't seem we'd stay that way for long. The other two men were now leveling crossbows of their own. They'd converged on us, clearly deciding that Drake was the more desirable target. Their plan seemed a good one if it involved puncturing my husband and then beating me to death.

I grabbed the footstool at my feet and chucked it at the nearest assassin's head. He reacted instinctually, his aim deflecting to the side as the bolt shot harmlessly through the tent's wall to our right. The second man aimed his crossbow and fired at the same time that Drake dove to shield my body with his, and luckily his momentum carried us clear of the kill shot.

Then the vicious struggle really began. I rolled onto my back as Drake got up, took a lantern from the table where we'd eaten our dinner, and prepared to fend off all three assassins, each of them having discarded their used crossbow to draw a close combat weapon of choice. One killer gripped a hatchet while the other two killers brandished curved, unfriendly-looking swords.

Drake was a magnificent fighter, but right now he was a magnificent fighter in his birthday suit. I needed to jostle the odds more than a little.

With a diversionary shriek I grabbed my ruby-studded belt and charged at the man with the hatchet. He sneered at me, probably not too intimidated by a naked woman with nothing but a belt in her hand. Then again, he probably wasn't aware of the throwing knives attached to that belt. I was having a hard time learning to train with throwing knives, and making me wear them at all times had been Drake's way of getting me to practice. I think he'd enjoyed it almost as much as me when we'd seen his mother's reaction to the scandalous idea of me wearing them at our wedding.

Looks like I would be getting some practice I hadn't bargained for.

I flew ahead like a banshee, my wrists flicking as I prayed that my flawed skills would be enough. The assassin didn't see the flash of the first knife in the moonlight and so he never tried to duck the blade that plunged between his ribs. He lurched forward with a painful grunt as my second knife caught him just below the sternum.

At the same time I was dimly aware of Drake's dance with shadows who moved, grunted, and then bellowed in dismay. One man dropped, disarmed and with an arm bent at an angle no man's bones should ever imitate. I heard his gurgled cry as the Black Knight ran him through with his own sword. Drake then dodged a thrust from the other sword-toting assassin as I emptied the rest of my knives his way, their veering arcs distracting him just long enough for Drake to outmaneuver him with a slice across the abdomen. There was a terrible cry, followed by a pitiable moan as an awful stench filled the tent.

By now we weren't thinking. Just moving. I doubted that my wedding gown would be the most practical armor and I didn't know how many other assassins might be waiting out there to make sure their friends had finished their task. So I just crouched low, still naked as a nymph, and retrieved two of my throwing knives from the first fallen killer. Then I tried to meet Drake's gaze so that we could agree on where to go from here.

The only problem was that our lantern had been destroyed in the struggle and everything was pitch black.

I didn't risk making a sound, not even a whisper. Drake had the same idea, but I felt his hand snag my wrist in the darkness and give it a tug.

After a few more heartbeats, with only the forest's sounds echoing around us, I heard his voice.

"Naji, are you hurt?"

It was probably stupid, but I lowered my arms as he enclosed me in a fierce embrace. His hands roamed across my face, shoulders, and back searching for wounds that luckily weren't there. My breasts felt the warmth of his chest, and it was all I could do to rip away and hiss at him. The arousal coiling though me was anything but helpful, and I cursed my traitorous body.

"I'm fine! Now let's focus!" I looked left and right. Beyond the beckoning tent flap the world seemed peaceful. So why were the hairs on the back of my neck giving the moon such an erect salute?

"Did you see that?"

"See what?" I asked.

"Those attackers were ambassadors," Drake said, fury rising in his voice. "I'll have the Knights who sent them regret the day they were born."

"I'm pretty sure that's an overused threat," I mumbled. "And besides, what's our exit strategy?"

Just then we heard movement coming from all sides of the tent. Skin prickled up and down my body, and I realized that so far all we'd done was give ourselves a little extra breathing room in which to die.

Chapter 11

I listened carefully for the footfalls of several, possibly a dozen men who meant to kill us. Perhaps I should have panicked, but right now the only distracting emotion I felt was anger. Anger that these men thought that they could murder two people in cold blood. I glanced at Drake, and luckily my husband hadn't been wasting time.

Underneath the bed lay Drake's great-sword with its lifelike dragon coiled around the hilt's bottom. Its gaping mouth seemed ready to spew acid or flame, and as Drake drew the weapon with a flourish it seemed as if the dragon might spread its wings and animate.

A man with a great-sword is a danger to anyone around him, and this weapon wasn't of ordinary make. It was one of the Black Knight's artifacts of power, a one of a kind magical item which Drake had inherited from a line of ancestors going back nearly 250 years.

Of all the Black Knight's enchanted objects, this was the only one which Drake always kept close, and now it was a good thing because it gave us a fighting chance. I was a weapon of sorts too, and I planned to give the odds an extra nudge in our favor.

The would-be murders outside must have gotten impatient because suddenly a deadly barrage of bolts punched through the tent at a variety of angles. I ducked low, my hands yanking Drake by the ankles to force him down to my level. He dropped the sword, losing his grip and cursing under his breath. I'd accidentally disarmed him, but that seemed a whole lot better than watching him become a human pincushion.

We pressed our bodies flat and kept our breathing quiet. For a few moments the harmless creatures of the night reasserted their dominance. The chirping of cicadas taunted us with a normalcy I knew was false.

Then the people trying to kill us made their next move. A column of shapes hurtled through the entryway. Four men ducked through the tent flap before Drake could react, but I slowed them down when the first throwing knife shot from the catapult that had become my arm, and it buried hilt-deep in one assassin's unfortunate eye.

I doubted he would ever enjoy reading a good book again. Definitely a fate he deserved.

The second knife slid from my fingers like an extension of my body. I knew before my eyes saw that it would find prone flesh. I wish I could've called it skill, but it was more luck which had the blade sinking into his neck. He stumbled, gurgling as he slumped over and looked down at his life seeping away.

The two unscathed killers split up and tried to avoid Drake's swipe with his head-seeking great-sword. The assassin whose eye I'd skewered was still clutching his eye socket and screaming when Drake lopped off his head as an accidental bonus. One of the two other assassins managed to duck underneath the swing, but his nearby partner wasn't so fortunate. Blood fountained as the great-sword nearly cut him in half.

I still had better things to do than gape at the gory spectacle, though, and my hands were already scrabbling for the fallen hatchet of the man I'd killed.

I saw the lone remaining assassin lunge at Drake with a short blade. The thrust should have gone through my husband's kidneys. Would have if Drake's sword had been just a sword. But the Black Knight was not just a man, and his fingers weren't gripping just any sword hilt. Heavy though a great-sword should have been, in Drake's fists the enchanted weapon became featherlight and moved like the nosedive of a falcon. It was hard *not* to be mesmerized by the way Drake reversed the blade to block the assassin's thrust. He made it look effortless. Even sexy.

In the faint shard of moonlight I saw the assassin's form, which was much larger than his recently slain friends. He sidestepped, barely avoiding a slash from Drake that would have spilled his guts.

"You can't win, Brother." At those words all combat froze. Drake and I turned to see two men still wearing their ornamental doublets from our wedding ceremony. They stepped into our spacious wedding tent as if they were healers making a house call. One of the main differences I noticed, though, were the seven additional assassins in ghostly camouflage who had surrounded us while we were distracted fending off the others.

I recognized Ecthor's voice first. Ecthor was the older of Drake's two brothers. His eyes were the color of amber, and in them I saw the unmistakable intent to kill. *Why?* I thought. *Of all the sick and twisted things...Kingdom's mercy!* Fraey stood beside him like a loyal twin, and though I saw a spark of regret in his face, I knew it wouldn't be enough.

The slender, slightly feminine face of Ecthor would have been pretty if it hadn't been contorted by so much hate. He and the other assassins raised crossbows in unison, proving that even heroic resistance can't get you out of every situation. Enchanted swords were great, but Drake was not a god and I certainly wasn't a goddess. At point blank range I wasn't optimistic about our chances, but I preferred to be productive and die trying. I snarled and prepared to get skewered while at least charging the despicable pigs who'd betrayed their own brother. The thought somehow haunted me—*What if their betrayal was because of me?*

I imagined how it would feel, those crossbow bolts carving a hole through my stomach. Maybe shredding my lungs. I prepared to feel pain in amounts I'd never known. But a curious thing happened. A surprised look painted Ecthor's face and Fraey's in two shades of puzzlement, and my jaw dropped when I saw each one fall clutching at a mortal wound. Bronwyn was standing behind them, now discarding two spent crossbows from her outstretched hands like a kitchen maid dispensing dirty dishrags. She efficiently unslung a third loaded crossbow from her shoulder, aimed, and fired.

While Ecthor and Fraey began the undignified process of bleeding out, one of the startled assassins went down with Bronwyn's third bolt tunneling through his chest. That seemed to cow the rest, including the broad-shouldered assassin whose blood Drake had tried to use for redecorating the tent moments earlier.

Mr. Broad Shoulders raised his hands high, his weapon gripped nonthreateningly.

"We surrender, lord. We put ourselves at your mercy."

The man knelt, tossing his weapon out of reach to prove his intent.

Bronwyn walked over to the two mortally wounded princes. She looked down at Ecthor and gave him a nudge with her foot. If I hadn't known better, I would've thought I saw a grin light up her face at the sound of Ecthor's agonized groan. Who knew my friend was also a bit of a sadist?

"Next time you try to assassinate a Knight and his Queen you might want to wear body armor. Just a suggestion," Bronwyn purred.

I doubted these men had planned on a female stable master violently interrupting their well-choreographed assassination. I looked at the young woman who called me her best friend, and the feeling was definitely mutual. If it wasn't before, it was now, as sure as rain was wet.

Drake approached the prone assassin who seemed to be their voluntary spokesperson. He rested the edge of the great-sword across the big assassin's throat and forced his head back until he had to strain to keep his neck from being sliced open.

There was something unreal in seeing my naked husband, his pectorals smeared in blood not his own, holding a weapon to a fully clothed man and demanding answers. My hand still clenched around my hatchet in a death grip. I watched, ready to brain any of the other six assassins if they so much as twitched in my direction. Wisely they followed their leader's example.

"Do you have a name, friend?" Drake's tone was deceptively casual, and he said the word 'friend' like it reeked of horse manure.

"I am Sawuli."

I could see Drake's eyes dart to his brothers, but only for a moment. The desire to pin them down and demand answers must have been savage, but the assassins were still the main threat. My husband kept his attention doggedly on them. *An unarmed enemy is not a defeated enemy.* He'd told me that in training often enough, usually after I'd disarmed him and still lost the match.

"Naji, go fetch Lady Vaela. We'll need her healing skills to keep those wretches from bleeding out."

What part of 'I'm naked' don't you understand? That's what I wanted to yell at the idiot who was my husband, but I realized that his priority right now was getting me to safety. He wasn't sure that the assassins here wouldn't have a change of heart, and he was willing to risk Bronwyn over me.

I couldn't blame him for that train of thought, but…actually yes, I could. It didn't sit well, the idea of my best friend's life being put in danger when it seemed more appropriate for me to stand by my husband's side. But that was an argument we'd hash out at a later time. Besides, *his* nakedness would've been too distracting at the moment to have that conversation anyway.

I leapt over to Bronwyn and gave her a bone-crushing hug. "Thank you for saving us." Bronwyn squeezed me back and kissed my cheek.

"Shush. You're a Queen now, remember? Saying 'Thank you' is unbecoming. Now go! Find Lady Vaela and the castle guards."

I vanished into the night like a memory. At least that's how I romantically pictured it as I leapt onto Bronwyn's horse and gave it a hard nudge in what I hoped was horse speech for 'Move like the wind!'

The beast obeyed me easily enough, and we began the climb up the steadily sloping field toward the Black Knight's stronghold. The stretch of field here was a finger between two patches of dense forest. The idea at the time had been to have the wedding ceremony surrounded by the musical rustle of the leaves, but now the tall shadows just looked ominous and added urgency to my aching limbs.

I stared straight ahead, focused on the vigilant glow of the fires along the castle's ramparts. They'd never looked so welcoming. I mentally groaned at the bedraggled sight I was about to present to the Captain of the Watch. Turdrin was a stoic, very proper soldier. The sight of his new Queen covered in assassin's blood and not much else would give him more than a little indigestion. I should have been worrying more about my surroundings, though, and less about how quickly Lady Vaela could be roused from a sound sleep. A creature abruptly came crashing from the trees like an avalanche.

It was one thing to hear of ogres in tall tales, but quite another to have one lumbering towards you at the speed of an arrow. I fell off the horse, my shriek cut short as a large hand gripped me by the throat, lifting me high. Moonbeams threw my face, chest, and extremities in a wash of pale light, but the shadows of the tall trees still hid my attacker's face.

Only by his height did I make the guess that he was an ogre, and when he leaned forward he erased all doubt. The ogre's handsome faces—yes, ogres had two heads as reliably as humans sported two arms or legs—peered at me intensely.

Both those faces were handsome, and the ogre's build was massive but otherwise just as glorious as any masculine physique I'd been told about as a child listening to my maid's far-fetched stories.

Both sets of eyes were a deep red. Just a point of fact, it's very hard to pull off red eyes without looking creepy, and this ogre was no more fortunate.

The creature's intense gaze made goose bumps ripple up and down my arms and even ripple across my breasts. My eyes must have been the size of moons, and fear was throttling me every bit as much as his massive hand. My own tiny hands and fingers were gripping the ogre's wrist, trying desperately to get him to loosen his hold. Each hard-fought lungful of breath came back out as a wheeze.

This was it. I was about to die. I didn't know much about ogres, but what I did know was that they weren't happy-go-lucky creatures. They didn't have a soft spot for humans, and if anything they disliked humans even more than trolls did.

I nearly soiled myself when one of the heads spoke.

"You must be Queen Najika, one of the two we were supposed to kill if you escaped your tent." The ogre said this so matter-of-factly it took my breath away. I probably made an odd face, because the ogre continued as if I'd offended him.

"What? You think that because your ridiculous myths depict us as savage brutes that it must mean we're dumber than a broken church bell?"

The second head interrupted his counterpart. "Najika, we have two brains to your one. Do the math. Does it make sense for us to be dumber than humans? Now we may not be twice as smart either, but we *are* your equal and more. Don't forget it."

I managed to speak as his hands relaxed around my throat. "Does this mean you won't kill me?"

The ogre heads gave me a puzzled look, and I realized that something had been lost in translation.

"Kahg doesn't understand." The head calling itself 'Kahg' looked over to the nearly identical and equally handsome head.

"Hahg also doesn't understand the human's point. We have been ordered to kill the Black Knight and his Queen if they should escape the death trap at their wedding tent. In killing you, we accomplish half our duty. What part of that involves you still breathing, woman?"

My mind was reeling. If the two ogre heads didn't kill me physically, they might frustrate me to death.

"Why talk to me if you are just going to kill me?" I cried.

Hahg snorted. "Because, silly human, it is always worthwhile to teach and instruct. This is the ogre way. Is that not right, Kahg?"

Kahg nodded solemnly. "An ogre is constantly learning from himself, and so it is right and good that he pass information on to others. Even those he is about to kill."

"Wait!" I begged. "Before you kill me you should know that the two men who planned this assassination are wounded and dying even now. Prince Ecthor and Prince Fraey have been captured and their assassins are either dead or held captive as we speak. There is no need to kill me. The conspiracy has failed. It's over."

Kahg and Hahg exchanged a conspiratorial glance. "Those two princes were just pawns, Najika. You and your husband have thwarted nothing. We still have no reason to let you live."

I was wracking my brain for what this could mean, and for any bargaining chip I could somehow produce out of thin air.

Then I remembered a fleeting scene from one of my maid's old legends. It was a far-fetched hope, but it was a hope. I had to believe that my maid's stories were based on at least an ounce of truth, didn't I?

"But you have every reason to let me live. I have been poorly treated by the humans in power, by the Knights of Arkor who hate you just as much as they hate me. Haven't you heard how I was unjustly condemned to die, and then sent away in disgrace? I have no more faith in humanity than you do, but some humans *are* better than others. I am one of them. I promise you, if you'll let me go free, that I will go to your people and make the Black Kingdom your ally. And if my husband has somehow wronged your people, I will make him see the error of his judgments."

I wasn't sure if my little speech worked, but I felt the ogre's grip loosen a fraction more.

"Why would we believe you, Najika? Humans lie all the time. A good human is usually a dead human."

"Because you're smarter than me. You said it yourself; you have two brains to my one. Look into my eyes, great Kahg and Hahg, and tell me if I'm lying. I have no doubt that with me naked and helpless in your grip, not to mention absolutely terrified, that if I were to lie to you right now, you would know it. You would *know* it. Wouldn't you?"

Here was where I had to pray that my maid's stories were right. Was their arrogance as towering as I hoped it was? As prone to flattery?

Hahg gave me a doubtful look. The left head turned to the ogre's right head. Kahg chewed on his bottom lip.

"The human woman does have a point. What exactly is your promise to us, Najika? Say the words, and be precise."

Hope flared in my chest like a fire being fed twigs with gale force winds surrounding it.

"I, Najika, Queen of the Black Kingdom, swear to visit your people within a week's time, to present myself before your leader, and to do everything in my power to prove to you that my husband and the humans of the Black Kingdom are the lesser evil. That we want, if not friendship, then at least an alliance which benefits both sides."

"And will you bring an army with you for these *negotiations*? Or will you come yourself, with just a few servants from your royal household?" Kahg and Hahg looked at me intently, and I knew this was where I could either screw things up royally or save my butt.

"I will only bring a few trusted advisors and servants. No one else."

Hahg slowly nodded, and Kahg grunted his assent. "Okay, human. We know you are telling the truth."

I could have been lying through my teeth, but it was good to know that my flattery and their arrogant faith in their intelligence made such a good team.

The ogre's hand slowly lowered me to the ground. They'd scared away my horse, and it looked like I would be hoofing it on foot the rest of the way to the castle.

"You will come north to the Cloudpeaks and talk to our people, Queen Najika of the Black Kingdom. We will be expecting you." With that the ogre crashed into the night as the tall, swaying grasses parted for his advance. I sat on the ground, my heart hammering through my chest like an ogre-sized drum being pounded.

My mind tried to make the connections. What could Drake's brothers provide that the ogres would want? Why would the ogres want to jeopardize the unofficial alliance that had existed between them and the Black Knight's household for nearly 250 years?

There would have to be time for answers later. I had a long sprint ahead of me, in bare feet in the dark, and I was definitely not looking forward to it.

Chapter 12

The setting sunlight shaved the horizon with a knife of peach gold brilliance. The sight should have brought poetic thoughts to my mind, if I'd cared much about poetry. Which I didn't. And even if I had, my mood wasn't helping.

Bronwyn, ever-faithful Bronwyn, was a soothing shadow which mirrored my every move. Unfortunately for her, that involved me stalking back and forth in front of the window and wearing a ragged ditch through the carpeting. My abrupt turns made following me difficult, not to mention rife with the possibility of bodily collision.

"I've told him everything, and what has he told me in return? Nothing!" I walked faster, biting my lip and fingering the hilt of my sword. I was wearing a hunting tunic and leggings underneath a leather breastplate and shoulder armor. They gave me a nice, lethal air. I had told the servants to ready my black chainmail, weapons, and warhorse just in case. If the conspiracy went beyond the princes, then who could be trusted?

"My Lady, I'm sure that the Black Knight will tell you everything once he has something he can verify. You must give him time to make contact with his sources. You know of his special gift—to see through the eyes of the spies he trusts who are spread all across the Kingdoms of Arkor."

When I sighed and fisted my hands in frustration, Bronwyn barreled on. "You know that he has taken the information you gave him and is using it well. Why are you so angry?"

I rounded on Bronwyn, and if words could blister mine certainly would have.

"What about Drake's interrogation of the assassins in *private*? There was no reason I could not have been there for the questioning! We are supposed to be in this together, Bronwyn. I am his *Queen*, not a wide-eyed girlfriend!"

I quietly wondered what Drake's methods with the assassins had been. Had he tortured them in the dungeons? It seemed likely. Regardless, I should have had input. I would have declared a resounding 'No!' to torture. Was that why he'd kept me out?

We'd barely been married a day, but I was already furious with Drake.

The double doors of the Black Knight's private conference chamber opened wide with a grand sweep. Sir Drake stepped out with several advisors flanking him like fawning little imps. I tried to remember their names, but couldn't. It wasn't very fair of me. They were good men. But right now I was in no mood to deal with them, and their braided white beards made me want to make bird's nests out of all their faces.

"Naji, please. Come." Drake gestured me into the conference chamber I'd seen only a handful of times.

When we stepped through I tried to ignore the feeling of awe that spread through my soul as I looked up. Above loomed a sky of ceiling tapestries depicting giant dragons spewing emerald fire at one-eyed monsters whose talons were longer than mountaintops.

Slowly my gaze came back to eye level and narrowed on *him*.

"I can see that you are angry with me, Naji."

"Lovely. It's refreshing to know that your amazing intellect can detect at least that much," I shot back with plenty of acid. "But to earn the true prize why don't you tell me *why* I'm angry, husband of mine."

Dressed in his court finery, a tight-fitting black doublet and hose with ebony-fringed boots, Drake cut an impressive figure. Yet the look he gave me was one of a child found with his hand in the cookie jar.

"Forgive me, Naji. I was trying to protect you from this…"

"I don't need that kind of protecting, Drake. It's your duty to stand by me, and to let *me* stand by *you*. I thought that's what this entire marriage, Knight-and-his-Queen thing was about." I gave him a gaze of steel that said if it was about anything else, he was going to lose a significant piece of his anatomy.

Drake put his hands up. "Okay, okay. This is the truth. The truth is that one of the assassins was cooperative. He'd been forced to take up the mission against his will, with his family held as collateral for the job. He doesn't trust them, though, and he decided he would rather betray his domineering masters and at least get some vengeance for the loss of his wife and children."

I quirked an eyebrow, suppressing a shudder. "He sounds like either a ruthless man or a snake willing to do anything to save his own skin. How do you know we can trust what he says?"

"Because what he says checks out with what I've been able to see through the eyes of my spies. *And* from what little I've been able to get out of my brothers."

My face softened at Drake's mention of his brothers. I saw the pain zigzag across his face as he referred to a betrayal that couldn't get more personal. Then I thought of my own family. Of my father, who'd torn open my heart the day I found out he would not try to defend me in front of the Conclave. Or the day I stood there as he let me nearly be condemned to die and then banished without a single protest.

"I'm sorry this has happened, Drake. Sweet mercy, I know there's nothing I can say." I crossed the room to him, cupping his tortured face between my hands and giving him a proper kiss.

As we drew apart, though, I sensed a reluctance in him. Whatever he was about to reveal, the idea of walking barefoot over a bed of needles seemed far more attractive to my husband.

"What is it? What did the assassin confess?"

"You want the short version or the long version?"

"Give me the short version and add in the really juicy parts," I said, trying to lighten up an awful situation.

"My brother Ecthor has secretly resented my place as heir to the Black Kingdom. For over a decade he has let his resentment fester, conjuring plots, until finally the spark came for him to act on it. My marriage to you meant that I might soon have heirs of my own. That his place in the royal succession would become well out of reach."

My hands clenched. That son of a...

"The fact that you were a princess from the White Kingdom we called our enemy made it even easier for Ecthor to delude himself into thinking that his personal ambition was a righteous cause. He convinced himself that I was being misled by a seductive temptress intent on stealing our Kingdom, that you would murder me and give the White Kingdom an opportunity to invade. In accepting you and making you my Queen, I am just as much to blame and just as unforgivable in his mind. Fraey followed Ecthor's lead, as he's always done—ever since we were children."

I took Drake's hand in mine, using touch for comfort. What else could I do?

"What I didn't count on, though, was that he would make contact with other enemies I least expected. The Red Queen and the Green Knight."

Drake must have seen me pale as my jaw clenched and my fingers swirled firmly around my sword hilt. I should have killed that woman. I should have killed the mother of the monster I first married. Lady Egwen.

Drake's hand strayed to my cheek, stroking it calmly as if to make the truth any more palatable. "Ecthor thought he was making a *deal* with the Red Queen and the Green Knight. The so-called arrangement was that they would send in assassins disguised as royal ambassadors from the other Kingdoms of Arkor. They would help Ecthor kill us and then place him on the throne, supposedly forging a new alliance."

I shook my head. The naïve fool. I almost said the words out loud, but then realized that trashing Drake's brother would only tear a new gaping wound in what were probably already raw emotions.

"I know, and what the Red Queen *didn't* tell my brother was that the assassins had replaced *real* ambassadors sent by all the different Kingdoms. By killing them discreetly near the border with the Black Kingdom and then disposing of their bodies, the Red Queen has left us as the primary scapegoat."

I was starting to see how the threads connected. My heart nearly froze.

"If what you're saying is true," I replied, "then the Kingdoms will not believe us when we say that *we* were not the ones who killed the ambassadors. They will see the slaying of the ambassadors meant to attend my wedding as an act of barbarity. They'll demand revenge."

Drake grimaced. "I'm afraid so. It means that we may see something we haven't seen in over 70 years. A combined army from all the colors, from every Kingdom in Arkor, united and determined on a retaliatory strike against the Black Kingdom."

I tried to sound hopeful. "But the Black Kingdom has weathered such invasions before, hasn't it? Some of the tragic legends I was taught as a girl in the White Kingdom tell of smashed armies on the black crags around the 'Kingdom That Has No Name.'" That was derogatory slang for the Black Kingdom throughout the rest of Arkor.

Drake shook his head sadly. "My grandfather was a young boy the last time we had to fight off such an onslaught, and back then it was *different*. Then we knew that the ogres would stand by us. But your encounter with Kahg-Hahg tells us that this isn't something we can count on. We need to find out why, and before it's too late. I've been taking their loyalty for granted for too long. The armies of all the other colors are already making the preparations for war. We don't have much time."

I chuckled, but there wasn't any humor in it. "So even if Ecthor had managed to kill both of us, he would've been washed away by the tide of the combined armies of the other Kingdoms at the Red Queen's urging. She would have used him as a scapegoat for the death of all the ambassadors, just as she's using us."

My husband gently took both my hands in his. We stood there, our eyes exchanging flickers of doubt and love, each of us trying to find strength from the other's example.

"I almost admire the old bat. She's a shrewd politician," I admitted, surprised that such words could come out of my mouth.

"I'll assume that doesn't mean you want her any less dead," Drake replied, giving me a dark grin.

I gave him a full kiss on the lips, then drew back with a dark smirk of my own.

Chapter 13

"If we're going to be travelling together for two days, dear, then you may as well make the most of it and talk to me."

This was my mother-in-law's fourth request, just couched in different vocabulary, at getting me to open up. She must not have thought me too bright. Like a merchant trying to sell me an overpriced piece of fruit, she thought that changing the name of 'apple' to 'delicious red thing' would somehow change my mind.

"And no, dear girl, I do not think you're stupid. I'm sure you heard me the first three times. I'm only hoping that my persistence will win out. You strike me as a stubborn girl—not that I'm complaining. I was just as stubborn at your age…" Could the woman read minds? I tried to filter out the insistent melody of her voice.

I glanced over at Lady Vaela, envious by what I saw. She wore a loose-fitting blue tunic and trousers which made her look far more martial than her typical ladylike wardrobe allowed. She had this imperious air to her, yet somehow managed to reveal kindness in the pull of her face. She reminded me of a goodhearted chameleon. Someone who could be what those around her needed her to be, in the time they needed it.

"Lady Vaela, look…"

"Please, call me Vae."

I sighed. She was going to make this journey as difficult as possible, wasn't she?

"Look…Vae." It seemed wrong to call my mother-in-law by a nickname. So incredibly wrong.

I swallowed and tried again. "Lady Vaela, I appreciate what you did for me back there. I know Drake is less than happy about the two of us leading this diplomatic mission to solidify the ogres' support."

Lady Vaela gave me a shrewd stare, her lips turning up. "I would call 'less than happy' an understatement, dear girl. Wouldn't you? I've never seen my son's face turn that shade of red before."

"What choice did we have? The ogres have a matriarchal society. You said it yourself, Lady Vaela. The ogre Queen is more likely to respect my authority than any other human. They dislike humans and human customs, and in making me Drake's co-equal as Queen, we're at least sharing the ogre custom of a powerful female ruler. If this mission matters, then I'm the one who needs to lead it."

Lady Vaela huffed. "You're speaking to the choir, Najika. I must admit, I was impressed by how quickly you grasped the situation. I also happened to overhear of your bravery in defending my son on your wedding night. I completely underestimated you."

The infuriating woman actually graced me with a radiant smile. I wanted to smack her with my gauntleted fist.

I rode horseback in full chainmail in the hot sun, cooking from the inside out. That probably didn't enlarge my patience, and the fact that Lady Vaela had subjected me to an eleven-month-long mother-in-law hazing ritual, treating me with the coldness of ice, didn't make me want to warm up to her.

But after the first eleven months, ever since her son proposed to me, well, she *had* begun to accept me. To thaw. Maybe that counted for something, and I couldn't forget what she'd done for me on my wedding night.

I scanned left and right, seeing nothing but wildflowers and crops thriving in the fields. This easy, flat part of the journey would last the better part of the day, but after that it was a rough road. The Rotting Hills stood between us and the ogre country in the Cloudpeak Mountains.

Bronwyn rode on the other side of me, wisely keeping quiet. I sensed her desire to disappear, but I think she felt that her presence might make me slightly less irritable, so she stayed and endured what I thought might become the most painful conversation in human history.

Then, as if I'd just jinxed myself by the very thought, it *did*.

"I will also be the first to admit, Najika, that I am more than a little curious. Did you and my son get a chance to, hmm, how shall we say…enjoy one another's company before being nearly killed?"

My face must have frozen in shock. I just looked at her. What else could I do? I guess, like every stereotypical mother-in-law through the ages, she felt the liberty to let loose whatever was in her priceless head.

"Am I being too forward, Najika?" She laughed, a full-throated sound of glee that made my skin warm.

"Oh, dear goodness. I think you've turned a shade of red I've never seen before either. I have to confess, that's what I was going for."

With a wink at me and a slight touch of the stirrups, Lady Vaela urged her mount forward and left me in sweet, sweet peace.

I stared at her back, open-mouthed, as Bronwyn timidly broke the silence.

"She's quite…different, isn't she?" Bronwyn ventured.

"That's one word for it. I can think of better ones." Uglier ones, too.

"But she does have a point," Bronwyn mused, teasing me with a little grin. "How was he…in bed? Or did you not get a chance to find out?"

I looked at my best friend in horror. "Is this how you speak to your Queen?"

But Bronwyn laughed off my outrage. "No, this is how I speak to my closest friend. I thought this is what you prefer?"

Her eyes were sparkling with mirth, and I was at my wit's end.

It was with relief that I spotted the lead knight in our escort signaling for us to stop near a stream ahead. It was time to give the horses a chance to rest and drink, and to stretch our aching limbs. I gave Bronwyn a look more menacing than a barrage of throwing knives as I dismounted and led my horse to the cool, glittering blue water. In all directions I could see the fringe of mountains that had sheltered the Black Kingdom for centuries, but to the north where the ogres lived the mountains looked a little more ominous. The sun's gleam on their snow-flanked tops reminded me of the glint of steel before a sword rammed into someone's chest.

It seemed far too quickly that we were waving goodbye to the last rolling green pastures. Hills poked up ahead and the suddenly uphill track was about as welcoming as a scolding matron. I tried to look at the bright side. Within a few leagues there would be some tree cover. I wouldn't have to bake in my armor. Sweat was pouring off my brow. Soon we would enter what my map informed me were the 'Eye-pecked Hills,' which came just before the Rotted Hills.

I turned to Bronwyn with a perplexed look. "Up ahead—the Eye-pecked Hills. Kind of an odd name, isn't it? Does it have some special meaning?"

"Special isn't the half of it, dear. Think 'lethal' and you're on the right track." I gaped at my mother-in-law. Lady Vaela had snuck up on me...*again.* For a woman of her years she had a mysterious knack for stealth. A shiver rattled my spine.

Up ahead, dark clouds hovered. Was there a storm coming? I squinted, trying to make my eyes like an eagle's.

"What are those over there?" I pointed to the distant clouds in the same instant that it dawned on me—those dark splotches weren't moving in the way clouds were supposed to move. They weren't clouds at all.

"Everyone, dismount! Shield formation!" The sergeant who served as leader of the 16 other knights escorting us waved his hands frantically.

"Come, ladies. No time to waste! You don't want your eyes and flesh pecked off your bones, do you? Come walk in the center here." Clearly no one had bothered to tell me about all the dangers of this journey, and I was starting to regret it. Now, as my eyes saw the hurricane of dark feathers and beaks rushing to meet us, I realized that I was seeing thousands and thousands of birds.

Their angry cawing filled the air like a howling wind, and I quickly dismounted, leaving my horse to one of the knights as I joined Lady Vaela and Bronwyn in the center of the hastily created formation. I saw the knights unstrap giant rectangular wooden shields from the sides of their mounts. Some were attached to poles which the men could use to extend the shield higher above their heads. They were long enough that for every man's shield, three or four bodies could huddle in safety underneath when it faced the sky. I was stunned to find myself at the center of something that reminded me of a well armored turtle snug in its shell.

In our little cocoon of protection, I felt safe. Of course that lasted only until the first crows reached us.

It was like a constant thundering. Like a thousand tiny clawed fists crashing all around us. I heard knights grunt with their exertions as the crows hammered us, one angry cloud after the next. Normally it took a great deal to scare me. This qualified as a great deal, and my ears were pounding with the sound of the blood pumping through my head and chest.

"What in the Kingdom's mercy are those things?" I asked, having to raise my voice above the angry cries to be heard.

Lady Vaela grimaced. "We call them suicide crows. The ogres think of them as guardians, and these hills are their natural habitat. Usually they're content to eat mice and worms, but when they see an intruder they immediately go berserk. They'll peck clean anything larger than a small dog. They don't like the idea of predators roaming in their territory."

I heard the rampaging crows slam into the shield wall. One slipped between a crack I could swear was too tiny for an insect to wiggle through, let alone a screeching crow. The creature lunged at my face, but my hand came up automatically, knife ready. I gutted the thing in one clean swipe. I kept my dagger out.

I planned to keep both my eyes intact, thank you very much.

"These ogres seem like such a friendly people. I can't wait to meet them," I said.

Lady Vaela graced me with another of her smiles, apparently enjoying my sarcasm.

"Not the nicest of pets, are they? If it makes you feel better, even the ogres have to be wary when they come through these hills. This may be a buffer zone which the ogres find to their liking, but suicide crows don't discriminate. They'll peck an ogre to death with the same dedication. Believe me. I've seen it."

Her words caught me a little off guard. I guess I'd always assumed, in the way that younger people foolishly do, that somehow Lady Vaela had always lived a quiet, happy life in her stronghold in the Black Kingdom.

What adventures had she been thrust into? What horrors had she seen? I had to view my mother-in-law in a whole new light of respect thanks to the way she walked beside me, totally unruffled while the dark clouds of death buffeted the shield wall on all sides like water seeking the weak points of a sinking ship. Some of the crows wormed their way underneath the bottom edges of the shields, but the knights quickly dispatched them with the slash of a sword or the stomp of a steel-toed boot.

It took forever to travel through the worst of the 'bird storm,' as I called it in my head. The horses became skittish, and they had every right to be. My lungs were able to take in air again once the horrible rending sound of talons scratching wood and beaks pecking at our defenses faded…then stilled.

I held my breath, listening. I heard the sound our feet trampling along the dirt track. The jostle of the shields as each knight held firmly to a unified pace. The horse in front of me flicked his tail and gave a snort which I imagined was a snort of relief.

"Is everyone okay? My ladies, are you all right?" The sergeant's voice rang out like a bell.

"Well enough, Sergeant. Your men were outstanding." At Lady Vaela's compliment every knight in the company seemed to march with a firmer step.

"We just do what we're trained for, Lady Vaela. You honor us with your compliment though." The sergeant turned now, his voice carrying easily to the middle of the column where we marched. "We will stay in this formation for the next hour or so. My mission is to get you to the edge of the ogre lands in one piece, and I aim to do just *that*."

Chapter 14

It was nightfall by the time I was able to eat anything besides cold meats and cheeses. My stomach was ready to start a war. I removed my chainmail shirt and leggings, stretching my legs to the tune of a loud groan. I probably made enough noise to waken a bear in hibernation, but no one threw me any dirty looks.

Everyone else was just as exhausted and just as eager for sleep. I felt sorry for the knights who had to stand guard. I made a mental note to ask the sergeant if I could help keep watch, although I knew what his answer would be.

I gratefully ladled some of the warm soup cooking over the fire after taking a bamboo bowl from the nearby stack. The hills spread below us in shadowy lumps in the fading light. Above me I could see an early moon, already full, and a cloudless sky which promised a glittering tapestry of stars for the rest of the night.

Bronwyn nudged me. "So? Are you going to ask her?" We'd talked about this while the knights had been making camp, but now I felt reluctant to bring it up. Lady Vaela sat across from me, quietly eating her dinner. She seemed lost in her own thoughts.

"Lady Vaela, my Queen has a question for you." I jabbed Bronwyn hard in the ribs and wished fervently that I had a better means to punish her.

"What is it, Najika?"

"It's nothing, really."

"Oh? The look on your face tells me otherwise. If the prospect of bringing up the topic puts that fearful pallor over you, then it can't just be nothing. Out with it. What do you want to know?"

I sighed, giving Bronwyn a dark look. She seemed to be collecting those from me lately.

"Well, I wanted to ask about your husband, Drake's father. What was he like? Drake never speaks of him."

Vaela's eyes clouded over with sadness. "Ahhh. Yes. He was a good man. Stubborn, but good. It probably made us a good match." A wisp of fondness swept over the creases on Lady Vaela's face. Then she focused on me with her eyes, and it was impossible to look away.

"Drake's father was a man born to lead. Our alliances with most of the races who live in the mountain ranges encircling the Black Kingdom…we have *him* to thank for solidifying them. The trolls, the ogres, the ape-men…they had been tentative allies, friends of convenience really. Drake's father was such a diplomat. I went with him on many of his travels. He was always traipsing around his Kingdom, wandering here and there. The man had wanderlust in his blood. He couldn't stay put even if all the wealth in the world were laid at his feet."

Lady Vaela's eyes fluttered and refocused, as if she was travelling back from a faraway dream.

"Diplomacy is a fragile achievement though, isn't it? The ogres have proven that. Ahhh, inquisitive girl. Look what you've done. You've gotten me blathering on like an old woman. Shame on you!" She smiled, and I smiled back. Suddenly I was glad she was here. I'd started this journey deeply uncomfortable about her joining me. The longer I spent time with her, though, the more time seemed to eat away at that discomfort.

"I didn't mean to pry."

"Nonsense. And even if you did, it's okay. I'm a mother-in-law. Prying is my duty. I might as well take it as well as I dish it out, don't you think?"

I had to laugh at that, thinking how unreal this whole situation had become. Tomorrow at sunset we would be among ogres, if all went as planned. Just then booted footsteps intruded.

"Ladies, forgive the interruption. A few words about tomorrow." The sergeant looked over us gravely, his beard dotted with food crumbs. Apparently we hadn't been the only hungry ones.

"Today was easy compared to what we face tomorrow." He focused his attention on me. "My Queen, I should tell you that—"

"Please, call me Naji or Najika. Every time you say 'Queen' it makes me feel like I've aged three decades." Abruptly realizing the insensitivity of my words, I glanced over at Lady Vaela. If she took offense, she had the grace to hide it.

The sergeant cleared his throat, noticeably uncomfortable. "Very well. Lady Najika, we have passed through the first border between the Black Kingdom and the ogre lands. Tomorrow we have one more barrier to cross."

He took a deep breath, as if fortifying himself for a leap. "The Rotted Wood lies ahead. It's an enchanted place, and the vines which grow there are all parts of one intelligent mind. We call it the Dreamgiver. As we walk along the path it will dull your wits even as it shows you images—the most alluring or compelling or downright fascinating things you've ever seen in your life. It will beckon to you. It will tell you 'Come, come' and show you promises which will make your heart pound. Don't listen to it. Keep your gaze firmly ahead. Put one foot in front of the other. That's the only way you'll survive."

A chill had spread over our little campfire. I reached my hands out, trying to find reassurance in the crackling flames.

"What happens if we step off the path?" I had a feeling I didn't want to know the answer. Then again, Father always said I had more curiosity than good sense.

"You'll be eaten. Very slowly. The vines wrap around you and secrete a digestive juice that very, very slowly turns you into mush."

"How slowly?" Bronwyn seemed more fascinated than horrified by the strange creature. It made me want to jab her again.

The sergeant ignored her question and hurried on. "Now, luckily we *do* have a backup plan...in case the creature does charm any of you." He patted the thick bundles of rope over his shoulder. "We have plenty of rope, and we're going to use it. We'll tie this around everyone's waists and to our mounts. If one of us gets carried away, the others can serve as his or her anchor. I've never lost a man on a mission, and I don't intend to start now."

"Have you ever lost a woman?" I asked. The sergeant's face turned cherry red as he realized his mistake.

"No, my Lady, I have never lost a woman either. I misspoke. Forgive me."

"There is nothing to forgive, Sergeant. I can see that before this journey ends we will owe you our lives many times over. I am eternally grateful." I nodded respectfully and it seemed to make him blush. Apparently the sergeant didn't handle flattery too well.

"You are too kind, my Qu— ...Lady Najika. I will do my utmost to keep all of you unharmed." With a proper bow, the sergeant turned and left.

Yet I was left wondering. Just what kind of images would this creature put in my head? What kind of monster could invade your very sense of reality? And, on top of that, what kind of monster could literally control an entire landscape? Although I tried to convince myself that it was the rocky ground which made it hard for me to fall asleep as night deepened, a quiet voice in my head said differently.

What if the Dreamgiver mesmerizes everyone? Are you sure you're strong enough?

Chapter 15

We got an early start, which was fine by me. I'd finally given up on the chainmail. My poor horse didn't seem pleased by the redistributed weight, but staying conscious in the saddle took precedent. I wore a black tunic and dark leggings with a leather breastplate. It was uncomfortably hot, but that was a far cry better than scorching. Bronwyn rode up ahead to talk with the sergeant. I imagined she was peppering him with questions about the Dreamgiver. What fascination she found in a creature of horror which lured and ate people, I couldn't guess.

When she finally dropped back, I couldn't resist. "So, are you an expert on the Dreamgiver now?

Bronwyn gave me a look of mock disdain. "Make fun of my curiosity if you want, Naji. To be honest I find it ironic."

"Find what ironic?" I turned in the saddle and squinted under the glaring sun.

"You, of all people, should understand that kind of curiosity. If the Dreamgiver is our enemy, then the more we know about it the better. It just so happens that it thrills my sense of curiosity too. I always thought of you as fearless, Naji. You certainly proved that in our escape to the Black Kingdom. But I always thought that your fearlessness meant you were always thirsting for knowledge too. I've always equated courage with curiosity. I see in your case that's not quite true."

I balked as her words sank in. "Are you calling me narrow-minded?"

Bronwyn was rebinding her hair, trying to keep the tendrils from becoming unruly as the wind whistled through the hills. "Did I say that? No, I think a better word for it would be...*boring*."

She laughed as I swatted her in the shoulder. "I could demote you to a scullion's assistant, you know. Have you cleaning dishes in the royal kitchens the rest of your life. How would you like *that*?"

"What's to keep me from simply breaking them all? No dishware, nothing to clean. Problem solved," Bronwyn replied merrily.

I rolled my eyes at her. This was certainly not a proper relationship between a Queen and her servant, but I didn't want a proper relationship. I wanted a friend, and in Bronwyn I had that. Royal titles would never mean anything compared to the bond we'd formed during the frightening days as fellow prisoners.

The horses climbed as the world tipped upward and upward. Soon I noticed that the knights looked as edgy as a cat in heat. Even the sergeant had a twitchy air about him, and he began pausing frequently, raising his hand for the column to halt. The sun was nearing its apex in the sky, and the hills on either side of us were crowned with vine-covered trees. Although I could tell the trees were there, I couldn't see even the speck of a single trunk, so thick were the crawling vines and the leaves that seemed to cover everything far from the path.

"Dismount! We make our preparations here. Gentlemen, ropes! I want everyone anchored. And be quick about it."

I took some coils of rope from the sergeant, deciding to make myself useful. My knot-tying skills were serviceable, and pretty soon we had ropes interlocking each person's waist. We started to look like a column of people who'd been tangled on purpose in a fishing net. We moved just about as awkwardly too. It's hard to appreciate the freedom to adjust your pace until you become hyper-connected to everyone around you so that even a slight change seems to inconvenience your neighbor and vice versa. It felt a little like walking through ankle deep mud.

I watched with fascination as the hills on either side got swallowed up by the vine-encircled trees. It looked like some type of ivy, though its ten-pointed leaves, each about the size of my palm, had a purplish hue that gave it an exotic appearance...certainly none I'd ever seen.

"This is it! We're in the Dreamgiver's territory now. Stay sharp!" the sergeant bellowed.

"Is there any reason the Dreamgiver hasn't swallowed up the road too?" I called out to the sergeant.

He gave me an irritated look. "The ogres keep the road tended. They're not affected by the Dreamgiver. We *are*."

Bronwyn whispered, "You could have asked me. The sergeant told me about a fascinating book on the topic. Something about how the ogres evolved living near the thing, and over time they developed an immunity to the Dreamgiver's ability. It sounds like an exciting read. Perhaps we could check the Royal Library for it once we get back?"

I was all for a good read, but this did not sound like one. What it sounded, more like, was that Bronwyn was eager to distract me from the fear steadily beating its drum in my chest. I looked up and saw trees groping ever higher, their branches strangled in ropes of ivy. The more I considered it, the more this entire forest felt more like a graveyard of trees than an actual forest. It looked as if the trees were withered, as if each was domineered by some awful parasite sucking away all the best nutrients.

I shuddered, though the shade from the branches hadn't made it that cold. And that's when it began.

One of the knights to my left suddenly screamed a name. A woman's name. He bolted toward the left, straining with all his might. I felt a sudden tug as his body's inertia pulled mine. We held fast, though. The sergeant patiently kept shouting at the man, and the men next to him shook him to try to wake him from his trance.

The knight kept calling out to a woman we couldn't see.

"Belaney! Belaney! You're alive!" Judging by the devotion on the knight's face, this Belaney must have been his wife. But all we could see, as far as the eye *could* see, were giant weed stalks and trees covered in leafy vines. The Dreamgiver had snagged its first victim, and it was haunting to see the yearning on the knight's face. Had his wife died in an accident? In childbirth? Had some illness taken her?

Whatever it was, this creature had him believing that she'd been brought miraculously back from the dead. A cold, hard knot formed in my stomach and my hand went to the sword at my belt. The worst of it wasn't just seeing the man's delusional yearning. It was to know that I couldn't do a thing about it.

"It's okay. We're okay," Bronwyn said. She reached out to squeeze my hand, the hand that I didn't have on my sword hilt itching to rip my weapon free and hack at something—anything— just to feel useful.

But it wasn't okay. I looked out, my mind going blank except for one all-consuming focus. By the roadside stood a man with a boyish face. A man who was a man, but just *barely*, grinned at me.

"Is that my little sister all grown up? Nice sword! I never imagined you with anything bigger than a letter opener, but it's nice to know you can surprise me once in a while." The young man's smile lit up his entire face, and his smiling eyes reached out to me.

"Gav?" I stared at my brother, dumbstruck. My brother was dead, wasn't he? Had been for what, just over two years? I had a fleeting memory of Gavriel, my older brother, lying underneath plush blankets. His skin had looked as brittle as yellowed parchment paper, his eyes sunken and unhealthy. The plague had swept through the White Kingdom like a wildfire. It had touched almost every family, and it didn't care whether your blood was royal or not.

Brother. I'd loved my brother so much. He'd been the best older sibling you could ever hope for. He'd always watched out for me, but at the same time he'd been willing to get into mischief with me too. A good older sibling had the best qualities of a parent with none of the tiresome drawbacks, and the willingness of a friend to get into trouble when fun made it worth the gamble.

Gavriel had been this anchor in my life, and before meeting Drake my last truly happy moments had been while he was alive. Suddenly my mind fogged over, and I couldn't remember...had he really died? Maybe not. Maybe Gav had somehow made it. Somehow come back to me.

I tugged gently on the rope binding my waist. I desperately wanted to get a little closer to him. Move toward the roadside. All I needed was a glimpse. Just a glimpse to see if it was really him.

"Naji? Are you okay?" Bronwyn's voice was like a distant echo. It didn't concern me. It didn't matter.

I cared so much about Gavriel that it seemed terribly selfish not to at least make sure he *hadn't* come back somehow. My mind traveled down strands of thought as if tugged by a shadowy finger.

Suddenly what had made sense no longer made sense. What seemed mysterious, the impossible, abruptly held promise.

Who were these other people, anyway? I glanced at Bronwyn, at the knights around me. They didn't know Gavriel. They had no idea what I had lost.

"You don't remember, do you silly girl?" The young man who was Gavriel called to me.

"Remember what?" I mumbled.

"Father. You don't remember his artifacts of power? Tell me you at least remember the White Staff of Wholeness."

I did. Growing up as a princess of the White Kingdom, my tutors had taught me about all the artifacts of power which my Father had inherited. The Staff of Wholeness was one of those artifacts, and it had the ability to resurrect anyone. To bring someone back to life. To bring an entire army back to life. But it could only be used once. Some artifacts of power were like that, and the Knights who had them guarded them jealously, never using them except if the entire Kingdom was in jeopardy.

"You can't quite remember! I see it on your face, Naji. You'll always be the sweet and clueless little sister, won't you? You asked Father to use the White Staff to bring me back to life after I died of the plague. Remember?"

I *did* remember. I also remembered the solemn look in Father's eyes. The pain, etched in newly created wrinkles on a haggard face set in stone. *"No, Naji. I cannot. This is only for the good of the*

Kingdom, and the good of the Kingdom is worth more than any one person. Even my dear son. Even your dear brother."

I gasped as the memory washed out. Then I saw Gavriel again. He was standing much closer now, his feet nearly touching the dirt path.

"You did it, sis. Your plea stuck with him. He relented finally. He used the Staff and brought me back. So naturally the first thing I wanted to do was come find my little sister. The one I felt awful for abandoning."

"You didn't abandon me," I whispered.

"Well that's not how *I* felt about it. You remember my last words to you?

"I'm not leaving you, Naji. Who else is going to keep you out of trouble? More importantly, who better to get you into it?"

No…it couldn't be like this. I had to be dreaming. And yet, my mind didn't process the concept of 'dream' anymore. Gavriel was standing right before me and he seemed so real. The glistening armor he wore and the tabard with the crest of the White Kingdom across his chest blazed proudly. It was unlikely, but it was possible. Father could have changed his mind. Maybe it didn't matter how long Gavriel had been dead. Father could have used the Staff of Wholeness to resurrect Gav. I wanted to believe it more desperately than ever.

Yes, my brother was alive.

I looked down at the restrictive rope looped around my waist, the knots holding me in place. The rope seemed like a cruel chain meant to control me, and I hated it. Despised it with a passion. Before I knew it I was drawing out my knife. I cut through the rope and ran. I ran towards my brother, who beckoned and turned away.

"Come, Naji. I know a shortcut through the woods. Father is camped nearby. He wanted to come and apologize to you for what he did. For what he failed to do." Those words spurred me on even more. Tears filmed my eyes.

I was distantly aware of odd voices in the background. People yelling. Were some directed at me? It wasn't important, though. I'd found my brother. Gav could escort me to the ogres easily enough. There was nothing to fear, and for the first time I felt like I could lay all my burdens aside.

I followed Gavriel as he waded through the foliage. "The path is a little ways through here. I'll show you. Here, take my hand." He turned back, his smiling face making my heart ache.

"I missed you so much. I think a hug is in order, don't you?" I said crossly. He replied with an apologetic shrug and another one of those perfect smiles. I reached my arms around to hug him close. I felt something firm enclose me. It felt good to feel his warmth. To know that I wasn't just dreaming all of this. His breath was warm on my cheek. His mouth whispered in my ear.

"I'm sorry, Najika. Forgive me."

"Forgive wh—?" I started to ask, but even as I did I realized that something was horribly wrong.

Arms shouldn't feel like deadened weights. Legs shouldn't feel like they're being squeezed in a torture device. I blinked as Gavriel melted away before my eyes, and instead of his face I saw a cluster of leafy vines writhing and swaying back and forth like a giant head. I looked down, saw networks of vines holding my arms and legs fast, wrapping me tightly like a present. I screamed as the swaying vine-thing rushed to meet me, enclosing my face and shoulders.

Chapter 16

The Dreamgiver had me in its embrace, and it was a green nightmare enfolding my entire body. My lips felt the awful, scratchy texture of the vines pulsating around my face. I could sense its liquid secretions around my head, and then as they coated my nose and cheeks. A tingling began wherever it touched skin. I wanted to scream, but screaming wasn't going to do much besides get gooey nastiness in my mouth.

"DIE! Die, monster, DIE!" I couldn't give the war cry points for originality, but for sheer enthusiasm it won my heart. Then I realized whose voice I was hearing. Bronwyn's.

I listened at the sound of hacking and my nostrils twitched at the smell of smoke. The vines around me shuddered as if they'd absorbed an impact.

Of all the prey which the Dreamgiver had sucked in and eaten over the course of its long life, I doubted that it had ever faced anything quite as tenacious or formidable as Bronwyn Raeythwick. The girl who seemed to have 'saver of Najika's butt' stamped invisibly on her forehead was hacking, slashing, and dealing damage with the zeal of a badger after a beehive's honey.

I only knew this because as the vines around my face slipped loose, I spotted her between two leaves. She was hacking away with a *flaming* sword in her hand. I needed her to teach me that trick if we got out of this alive.

"Let her go!" Bronwyn roared like a lioness and the fiery sword bit through another chunk of vines. Each time tendrils of greenery tried to grab her, the heat from the fiery sword forced the creature to shy away instinctually. Bronwyn had become an oasis in a treacherous land of green death, and the gap between us was shrinking.

I managed to free one hand as the vines continued to loosen. Bronwyn's courageous stand was distracting the Dreamgiver, and I needed to take advantage. I managed to get hold of my sword, drawing it out from its sheath with a satisfying hiss.

Since the Dreamgiver felt the need to entangle me in a nightmare, it felt only appropriate that I wanted to become *its* worst nightmare. I inserted the sword behind the green vines still holding my other arm in its grip and began to saw back and forth, feeling a huge rush of relief as the sword gnashed through the tender green roots. My other arm shot free and I began sawing frantically at the vines around my legs. It took effort enough that my muscles protested, but first one and then the other leg shook free. I glanced over to get my bearings, and my heart sank when I realized how far from the road I had strayed.

I thought I was no more than a stone's throw away from the path. I was wrong.

"Najika! Come to me!" Bronwyn's voice filled me with hope as she slashed her way closer to me. The flaming sword whirled and flashed. The trees towering around us pulsated with vines, though, and some of those veins now ripped free of the tree trunks to lash out at us like the lolling tongues of a hideous beast.

It was too much, even for Bronwyn. I saw her slice a wriggling vine clean through, but in the next instant vines from the trees around her bore down on my friend from all sides. They scooped her up by her feet, avoiding the heat of the sword, and then the sword slipped through her fingers. Dozens of vines moved to smother the blade's fire, snuffing it out in heartbeats. Bronwyn's scream as the vines enfolded her carried through the woods.

"Run, Naji! Run!"

My feet wanted to run, but the broken part of my brain that apparently had forgotten the concept of fear wouldn't allow it. I ran towards the upside down figure of the girl who was like a sister to me. *I'm not leaving you, Bronwyn. Save your noble sacrifice for someone who doesn't give a damn. Because I do, and I won't sacrifice you. Your life is every bit as important as mine.*

I roared a battle cry of my own as my sword cut a satisfying gap through several layers of swaying vine that stood between us. I swung again, seeing red as clear juices splattered me. If this was the Dreamgiver's version of blood, I wanted more of it. I kept swinging, only dimly aware of the swirling vines detaching from the treetops beside me, rolling downward like a wave crashing against the beach.

I had just succeeded by some miracle to slash my way to Bronwyn's side when the rolling carpet of green death swallowed us both up, encircling and squeezing us like a jealous lover. I didn't scream at first as the vines covered my face. I knew when lost was lost. I tried to blot out all the tingling sensations and focused instead on the one good thing I knew. At least we'd taken a stand together. I wouldn't have to worry about survivor's guilt, wondering if I could have saved Bronwyn.

Be thankful for small blessings, Father had once told me. I tried to take comfort in that now as I closed my eyes and wished for sleep. How did this work exactly? Would I have to be conscious the whole time the Dreamgiver slowly digested me? The thought sent a tremor through my body, and the strong Naji melted, replaced by real panic. And then I screamed. The digestive juices pouring into my mouth didn't matter. I just screamed.

I could accept death. That happened to everyone. But to die like this? To have my best friend die in this same way, in gradually progressing agony? It was terrifying, and I couldn't handle it. Suddenly every second as the tingling on my skin progressed towards a burning sensation made my heart pound harder and harder, a stampede that made me feel like all my ribs were about to shatter.

I'm sorry, Drake. I failed you. I failed our Kingdom. I almost laughed, that's how far gone I was. *I'll probably go down as the*

Queen with the shortest reign in human history. It had been a few days since we were married, since I had become Queen of the Black Kingdom. Not that it meant anything now.

A fierce gale whipped through the trees. I couldn't see it. I couldn't *see* anything. But I felt it. Like a brewing storm, the very pressure in the air seemed to change. Then there was a vast buffet of wind, and I felt the vines enfolding me shake with the blast of force. That's when I heard...something. A bloodcurdling scream that wasn't human, wasn't *anything*, not anything familiar. It was like the roar of a thousand different beasts mixed into one earthquake-epic rumble, and it came down on the forest like a hammer.

I felt a surprising heat warm the front of me. My eyes popped open and I gasped with shock as the vines drew back from my face. The scene in front of me looked like I'd been tossed abruptly into a different world. Entire trees had been uprooted and discarded like toys during a child's tantrum. A solid sheet of fire coated the trees deeper in the forest. Vines crackled and burned, turning to ash as the flames raced along the roots, eagerly consuming everything.

The rest of the vines unfolded from me, shivering with what I imagined was fear, maybe despair, maybe both. I found Bronwyn barely conscious. She'd been enfolded in more vines than I had, and the pallor of her skin glistened with the Dreamgiver's disgusting secretions. I threw her arm around me and struggled to get us both upright. It was all I could do just to turn us in the right direction and propel us forward without tripping over a random root and sprawling headfirst.

"Stay with me, girl. You're not allowed to die on me." Why I said those words, I don't know. Similar words hadn't helped my brother. I guess they were more for me to say them than for her to hear.

We stumbled through the undergrowth. To keep her moving took every ounce of energy I had left. We moved like a man with a few too many goblets of ale in him, but at least we moved. The fires behind us raced and blossomed throughout the forest like a deadly flower. I had to admit, I kind of liked it.

What had created it, though? As I heard that bloodcurdling roar again, my eyes swept upward. I almost froze at what I saw.

Since I was old enough to hear stories, I'd always been fascinated by one legendary animal more than any other. Dragons. They weren't supposed to exist, but some of the old stories insisted they did.

Whoever had written those old stories deserved to tell everyone off with a really big 'I told you so!' because up in the sky, its black scales glittering in the sunlight, a black dragon swept in a graceful dive. I held tight to Bronwyn as the massive beast skimmed the air just above us, his screeching roar joined by gouts of flame that set the trees on either side alight like enormous torches. The big guy was literally our savior, but after leaving his mouth those flames didn't answer to him. Or to anyone for that matter. Getting burned to death also wasn't on my wish list of ways to die, so I lurched forward again, grimly willing Bronwyn to hang on.

The rest of the trek back to the road was just a blur. I remembered a knight's supportive arms helping us over that last threshold. Then I blacked out.

Chapter 17

Hands gently smacked my cheeks. Cold water rushed from a cloth being wrung over my face. My eyes fluttered open, and I coughed.

"Lady Najika. Lady Najika. Can you hear me?" I recognized the sergeant's voice. The chaotic blur in front of me coalesced into something solid. Okay, I could see and I didn't hurt all over. That was a definite improvement.

"Bronwyn," I croaked. Looking over, I saw Lady Vaela tending to a girl lying on the ground. At least Lady Vaela was a healer, and she could get Bronwyn on the mend. I tried not to think of the alternative. I sat up on my elbows. From the distance I could still hear the dragon's roars. Every now and then a new gout of flame erupted in the forest, spreading and licking at the treetops. I looked around and estimated that there were twenty, maybe more of these spreading infernos. It was like a web of fire had been thrown over the forest. What wasn't in flames soon would be.

"She looks okay to me. I don't think the secretions had enough time to do any lasting damage." That was the sergeant's assessment as he talked to my mother-in-law. Once she had Bronwyn resting comfortably she came over to me. For some reason she had a distant way about her.

I gestured at the roaring, fire breathing thing of majesty in the distance. "That was good timing. I'm assuming he's on our side?"

Lady Vaela gave me a cold stare. Something was definitely wrong. Why was she looking at me like that?

"What?"

"You don't know what you've done, do you?"

I put a hand to my forehead, willing the pounding there to give it a rest. A surge of anger replaced my relief.

"You want to tell me what you mean, Lady Vaela? Last time I checked I nearly got digested by a creature out of anyone's worst nightmare, and for all I know Bronwyn might not fully recover. If you want to lash out at me, do it with a little more class. Now what are you talking about?"

I'd never spoken to my mother-in-law like that. I couldn't believe those words had even come out of my mouth.

Lady Vaela shot back, unperturbed. "My son must have been watching through your eyes. He uses that ability, especially when someone he loves is on a dangerous journey. At any time of day he can see through the eyes of people he trusts. He saw that you were going to die *through your own eyes*, and he summoned the black dragon. He used his most cherished artifact of power, and it can *never* be used again. That dragon will tear down that forest and destroy every last shred of it, and then it will disappear, Najika. It can be used only once, and Drake just used it to save *you*."

I thought back to the black dragon on the pommel of Drake's great-sword. It had seemed so lifelike, so poised to leap out and spread its wings. Its dormant form must have been a tiny version of its true self.

"Are you talking about Drake's great-sword?" I asked.

"Yes!" Lady Vaela shouted. "He used it. He summoned the only champion that could have saved the Black Kingdom from invasion if we became so desperate. That was our safety net if the ogres had failed us. And now not only has my son used it up, but he's ensured that the ogres will become our enemies."

"Hold on." I put my hands up, the pounding in my head receding, but not enough. "You're going way too fast for me. What do you mean?"

"The ogres revere the Dreamgiver. They're immune to it, so they can afford to worship it as a god. They see it as a protector. Now we've just murdered it, and the ogres will blame us." Lady Vaela's eyes sharpened into spear points. "By rushing off headlong into the Dreamgiver's welcoming arms, in one stroke you've managed to destroy any hope we had for preserving the Black Kingdom. The combined armies of the other Kingdoms will come, and when they do what hope will we have? Now if you'll excuse me, I have a wounded girl to look after."

She swirled like a departing storm and left me, dumbstruck, to ponder her words. The sergeant gave me a sympathetic look, his hand resting on my shoulder.

"You'll have to forgive her, my Lady. She has a great weight on her shoulders. She's no longer the Queen, but she still thinks like one. Takes her Kingdom's welfare and her son's welfare very personally."

I glanced up at the sergeant. I swiped at the stupid tears slipping down my face. How had I messed everything up? Maybe it *had* been all my fault.

If Drake hadn't married me, his brother Ecthor wouldn't have had the excuse he wanted to rebel. If Ecthor hadn't rebelled, then the conspiracy with the Red Queen would never have happened. And if the Red Queen had not arranged for those assassins to kill and replace the ambassadors from the other Kingdoms of Arkor, then Drake and his people wouldn't be fighting for their lives, waiting for an invasion launched by the Knights from all the other Kingdoms.

All roads of fault lead somewhere, and that somewhere was *me*.

We didn't try to soldier on and make for ogre territory that day. Instead we camped that night on a hilltop crowned by boulders large enough to provide convenient shelter. During my time blacked out the knights had gotten us onto the horses and made good distance to get us clear of the forest path. We now had a breathtaking vantage point on our hilltop as the sun glazed the dimming sky. Brighter than the waning sun, I could also see the walls of flame dancing in the distance. The fires seemed to eat away merrily at the forest like a starving newcomer at a holiday festival.

I sat still, my legs tucked up to my chest, just staring. Staring as if I could find comfort in the flames.

"This wasn't your fault, Lady Najika. It was mine."

I whirled to my left, peering at the sergeant's face. *Go away.*

"It's been getting smarter. I should have taken it more seriously sooner. Maybe if I had, none of this would have happened."

"Look, I don't know how you even think you know what's going on in my head Sergeant, but—"

"Forgive me, my Lady, but this needs to be said. It doesn't take a scholar to see that the haunted look in your eyes comes from guilt. Oh, and by the way, you not accepting a single bite for dinner was also a pretty good clue. I am a soldier who follows orders, my Lady, but I'm not stupid."

I gave him a dark look. This was the last thing I needed right now, the sergeant growing a backbone and ignoring his Queen's orders.

"If I told you to leave me in peace, would you?"

"Not until I've said *my piece*," the sergeant replied. "The truth is that the Dreamgiver has been getting smarter. Bolder. When I was a knight just come of age we could walk that path and get no more than a few fleeting images. A few temptations here and there. But we resisted it. As time went on, the Dreamgiver's images became more lifelike and more of my men were tempted. I devised ways to cope with it, though. The rope system worked well enough. Has for years. I underestimated the thing, though. The Dreamgiver pulled you in, but it was able to do it while still letting your conscious mind perform complex tasks. Tasks like cutting a rope."

The sergeant grimaced. He sat beside me, then, and his hands pressed over his crumpling face.

"That was new to me, my Lady. Today I saw the Dreamgiver learn its next new trick and use it on you. I should have been prepared. I knew it was intelligent and that it could learn. I should have at least warned everyone. But I didn't, and you know why? Wishful thinking. I'd become set in my ways, believing that the same strategy would work again just because it worked before."

His hand clenched around my shoulder, forcing me to lift my face and see his anguish.

"It was my job to protect all of you, Queen Najika. To keep you safe. I failed. *I* failed. So, if you want to find blame, this is where it belongs. It belongs here." He pointed a finger at his heart. I wanted to protest, but that protest died in my throat when I felt his fierce conviction hitting me like an aura.

My thoughts collided, part of me not knowing what to believe anymore. Then a tiny voice in my head tried something else.

How much does it matter whose fault it is for what? Will it save your Kingdom if you find out? Wallow in hopelessness some other time, when lives don't hang in the balance. Some things have been lost, yes, but you aren't dead yet. Your husband loves you very much.

He sent a dragon to save you and used up his Kingdom's most precious resource. Are you going to throw all that away?

Sometimes I made a really good argument, even with myself. Sometimes I actually listened to myself too. I leaned over and kissed the sergeant's cheek, my hands gently resting on his shoulders as I stood up.

"Whatever fault you think is yours, I forgive you Sergeant. I'm turning in for the night. Time to see what sleep I can get, the kind not laced with nightmares preferably." With a firm nod I walked away.

Chapter 18

"Sir Kennian." I caught the knight's attention. It was his turn on watch, and everyone else slept in huddled lumps by the fire. His tired eyes tried to firm up as he snapped to awareness. I was wearing my night gown instead of armor mainly because I couldn't be too obvious about what I was about to do, in case anyone else woke up and saw me. I could hardly believe what I was about to do, anyway. Sometimes the only move was a drastic one.

"I wonder if I might have a word with you, just for a moment." The knight didn't seem suspicious. To the contrary, he seemed flattered that I wanted to speak with him. I set him at ease using the best way I knew how.

"Are you a bachelor, Sir Kennian?" The knight sheepishly nodded. He was a young man, maybe a year or two older than me at most. His face was clean-shaven and his eyes lacked the world-weary quality I saw in more seasoned fighters.

"I have noted your bravery during the journey. A man like you isn't easy to find. There is a noblewoman in the White Kingdom, a friend of mine whose family is very wealthy. Lady Palanai. I think she might make a good match for you." I told a half-truth there. I did know a Lady Palanai. Her family was fabulously wealthy. We *weren't* friends. More like frenemies...unless you counted her conceited parents' friendship with my father as a friendship by proxy.

I sighed. Might as well get this over with. Time to gauge his interest and see how bribable he was. "I was hoping you might tell me more about yourself. I was planning to write Palanai a letter, and your name might come up."

The knight gave me a rueful smile. "My Queen, I cannot thank you enough for the compliment, however I—"

"Please, call me Najika."

"Err...Najika. Look, my Lady, it is kind of you to offer, but with our Kingdom soon to be at war with all the other Kingdoms, I think it highly unlikely that any lady of her standing would be interested in a man whose Kingdom is her sworn enemy. The White and Black Kingdoms have never been friendly, my Lady."

"And yet here I am, wedded to your lord." I gave him a bold look. My dignified stare silenced him, and then I went on. "I have a plan which requires your help. You must tell no one and do exactly as I say. The alliance with the ogres depends on it."

Sir Kennian looked at me gravely. We seemed to both become suddenly aware of the sleeping figures bunched around the embers of the campfire not far off.

"Lady Najika, I'm not sure what you mean. I have strict orders."

"And I am countermanding those orders, Sir Knight. Will you listen to your Queen or to a sergeant?"

The man licked his lips several times. He looked like a mouse caught between two pieces of poisoned cheese. "My Lady, I really don't think there is much we can do this night."

I knew the only chance I had to salvage this mission, but for my plan to work I had to at least find the ogres in a receptive mood. I had promised Kahg-Hahg, the ogre I'd met on my wedding night, that I would show up alone except with maybe a few advisors and servants.

The original plan was for the knights to leave us at the border. But after all that had happened, I'd overheard the paranoid sergeant giving orders to his knights. They were to escort us all the way to the ogre Queen. That meant me breaking my promise to Kahg-Hahg. Whatever faults the ogres had, it seemed to me that promises meant something to them. I sensed that this was one of the reasons they disliked humans so much. We broke promises as easily as a piece of bread.

"I need you to leave with me right now. I must proceed to the ogre camp *this instant*. We are leaving and we are doing it in secret. I command this as your Queen."

Sir Kennian gaped at me for a moment before he recovered. "With all due respect, my Queen, your safety is the responsibility of the knights of the escort guard. We are under the command of

Sergeant Herveth. In this regard I'm afraid I must stick to my sergeant's orders."

"That would be a pity," I replied, my voice laced with steel. I slowly drew my sword. Hopefully he wouldn't call my bluff.

"What are you doing, my Lady?"

"I have an agreement with the ogre Queen," I lied. "If I do not show alone, she will be greatly displeased, and what slim chance of alliance exists will be torn away. Either you obey your Queen or you destroy the very purpose of this mission. That makes you my enemy."

I advanced on him, and Sir Kennian's hand strayed to his weapon, but he couldn't quite bring himself to draw it.

"You have two choices, Sir Knight. You may help your Queen complete this mission. I think any Queen would reward that most handsomely. I think a noblewoman like Lady Palanai could be easily convinced that a man of your courage might make a good match. Or..." I spun my wrist, letting the steel of my sword flash in the moonlight. "Or I will attack you, and you will have no choice but to turn on your own Queen and forever be dishonored for it."

The young knight put his hands up, palms out, and began to back away. "Please, Lady Najika, this is insane! Can you not simply convince the sergeant of the importance of what you just told me!?"

I shook my head. "No. After the disaster at the Rotted Wood he cannot be trusted to see reason." Also, he would know I was lying about the arrangement with the ogre Queen, but I neglected to point that out. "We must leave now, in secret, and you will not wake the next man for his turn at the watch. Now is the choosing time, Sir Kennian. Will you betray your Queen or will you show true courage?"

When the indecision on his face snapped, I could finally breathe.

"I am up to the task, Lady Najika. I hope you know what you are doing."

Me too.

Four hours later I stood with a young knight looking over the steepest descent I'd ever seen in my life. It looked so treacherous that we both gasped as we rounded the curve in the road.

"We might as well jump into a pit of tar. It would be an easier way to die," I mumbled.

"I'm sorry, what did you say my Lady?" I waved away Sir Kennian's question. We had made good time despite the fact that we'd had to walk the road's treacherous potholes largely in the dark. Dawn glistened along the outlines of the peaks in the distance. Time was not our friend.

It took us three more hours, and the sun stubbornly rose to announce morning by the time we reached the foot of the sandstone cliffs. We were now officially in the valley of the ogres, and I hastily put on my chainmail armor before telling Sir Kennian it was time to part ways. I gave him a kiss on the mouth which probably sent heat from his toes to the tip of his nose, at least if his reaction was any clue. I realized that if I was wrong about this and got myself killed, then he'd be dishonored. The poor man deserved more than a goodbye wave.

Then I mounted my horse and rode until that familiar baking feeling told me that this chainmail armor would have been the perfect culinary tool for cannibals. I wasn't sure whether I'd be cooked medium or well done by the time I arrived. Sweat poured off my forehead, trickling into my eyes as I swiped at it again and again. I was just getting ready to stop for a few swigs of water from my flask when I saw him. His two familiar heads peered over a boulder as tall as my horse.

"Kahg-Hahg, is that you?" I made sure that I was actually seeing the same ogre from my wedding night. Twin sets of red eyes studied me as he urged frantically for me to come as if I were a teleporting sorceress here to do his bidding instead of a Queen. I dismounted and led my horse through the tall grass, finally basking in the shade of the boulder. My guard was up though. The last time we'd met the ogre with two heads named Kahg and Hahg had nearly strangled me. I drew my sword out, ready for anything.

"You'll have no need for that, silly human woman."

"I *am* the Queen of the Black Kingdom. A little respect wouldn't be totally unreasonable."

Hahg produced a stiff upper lip, but Kahg sighed. "We do not mean to insult. We actually have been watching lookout to see if you would come as you promised. When we saw the Dreamgiver burning all through the night, we guessed that maybe it was your doing. Was it?"

I nodded, because in a way it was. "What of it?" I was worried how they'd react. I remembered Lady Vaela's words. To my shock, they just shrugged.

"That's your reaction? I've been told that ogres worship the Dreamgiver like a god."

Kahg-Hahg smirked at me. "Who told you that?"

"The former Queen!"

Kahg-Hahg chuckled. "We used to, sure. Religions can change, silly human. The Dreamgiver was demoted from god to monster by the last reigning ogre priestess nearly 30 years ago. Tell your former Queen she needs to read fewer books and get out more."

I tried to form words, but my heart was too busy jumping up and down with relief.

"Listen, Najika. We will tell you the truth because you proved yourself. You said that you would come without an army or men carrying weapons. You were true to your promise. You also said that you would come to talk of a lasting treaty. Is that still true?"

"That is the *only* reason I came. I want the ogres and the people of the Black Kingdom to have a real relationship."

Kahg-Hahg waggled their sets of eyebrows at me and smiled. Smiles were supposed to be comforting, but their blood-red eyes ruined the effect. "You do show a supply of courage, then. I hope you are ready to use it."

Kahg looked at Hahg. "Do you want to tell her or shall I?" Hahg threw his fellow head an irritable frown.

"Why do I always have to give bad news? It is your turn." Kahg rolled his eyes but surrendered.

"Your salvation and your worst enemy can be found in Agtha-Selene. She is our ogre Queen."

"My salvation and my worst enemy?" I echoed. "Is that supposed to be a riddle?"

"No," Kahg continued. "It is literally the truth. The Queen's left head calls herself Agtha. She is in league with the Red Queen and ordered me to help the assassins kill you on your wedding night. The Queen's right head calls herself Selene. She is interested in making a formal treaty with you and your husband. She ordered me to observe you and give my opinion on whether you could be trusted."

I gaped at him. "Wait. So you're saying that—"

"I have been forced to play both sides, Najika. One Queen tells me to kill. Another Queen tells me to be hopeful for friendship. It is no way to live." Kahg and Hahg exchanged commiserating glances like two boys without girls to dance with at a wedding feast.

I stifled a frustrated scream, settling for an anguished groan. "What am I supposed to DO?!" How am I supposed to kill an enemy conjoined to a potential ally?"

Hahg shrugged unhelpfully. "You're the Queen. I'm just a lowly warrior."

I wracked my brain for everything I knew about ogres. It wasn't much. It couldn't have filled a tiny children's book.

"Tell me this. Does one of your people ever lose a head? I mean, what happens? Can an ogre survive with just one head?" The question seemed ridiculous, but I had to ask. It didn't pay to assume. I'd learned that during my past year in the Black Kingdom trying to reorient my ways to a different culture.

Kahg-Hahg nodded in creepy tandem. "It happens. Sometimes there is a hunting accident. Sometimes two ogres fight, one loses a head. We usually follow the rule of a head for a head. But for Queens, rules are hazier."

"Is there some way I could challenge her to a battle?" My mind was racing, wondering if I could target Agtha during the fight and then concede *after* I'd killed the proper head.

"You could," Hahg admitted. "This is an ancient right. As the leader of your people, in theory you could challenge her. This is an ancient custom, that Queens may challenge one another."

"Why do I still see 'problem' written all over your foreheads then?" I said, crossing my arms and giving them the frown they so richly deserved.

"Because, Najika, Queen Agtha-Selene is several heads taller than you. The boulder you're shading yourself under now? She could lift it with her pinky."

I knew an exaggeration when I heard one. A wicked idea dawned in my head, and I couldn't help smiling anyway. "You let me worry about that. There's only one thing I need from you. Well, make that two."

I whispered to Kahg-Hahg, and both faces went rigid. "The first we can do, my Lady. The second will be…harder."

"But you can do it?"

Kahg-Hahg rubbed his hands together. "You are talking to an ogre spy. Trust me, puny human, I can sneak you in anywhere." He looked down at his leggings, then made an apologetic shrug. "Well, maybe not *anywhere*."

Chapter 19

Everything had worked out as well as I could expect, but that didn't mean this was a good idea. Kahg-Hahg had managed to convince the Queen's bodyguards to grant me a private audience. After the destruction of the Dreamgiver the ogres were all a little jumpy, and the murmurs rattling the great hall as I took responsibility for it gave me a wicked satisfaction.

Finally, when the niceties were all said and done, I stood facing the most powerful non-human leader in Arkor. She rose from her throne and walked towards me. I first focused on the left head, Agtha. There was a ruthless way her eyes seemed to size up the world around her. That set her apart from the ogre head named Selene, who looked to be by no means a pushover, but seemed to favor shrewdness over ruthlessness.

Both heads were blond, and both faces were beautiful. It felt strange to think it, but this ogre Queen really was a gorgeous woman—just not in the way humans would believe. The whole nine-feet-tall, two heads, and red eyes package didn't exactly conform to human stereotypes of beauty.

"So you are the upstart princess from the White Kingdom who torments us with these petty demands for fancy pieces of paper which mean nothing!" Agtha snarled, a veiled insult at the notion of any treaty.

Selene gave her fellow head a dismissive sideways glance. "She is a Queen now, or hadn't you heard, Agtha?" She spoke to her other self with a disgusted tone, as if she knew Agtha's words were just theatrics. Deep down I still felt like only a princess, but I wasn't going to tell *her* that.

Only Kahg-Hahg remained in the cavernous great hall with the Queens. It was a huge three-story structure with vaulted ceilings. A mouse could pass wind somewhere in here and still create an echo.

"Queen Agtha-Selene, I challenge you to a duel to the death."

The Queen's sets of eyes narrowed, one in rage and one in curiosity.

"I can explain, Your Highnesses," Kahg-Hahg interrupted, rushing forward and placing a piece of scented parchment underneath Agtha's nose. She looked down to read it, but no sooner had she looked, the substance coating the paper imparted its noxious fume. Agtha's nostrils widened as she coughed and then passed out. *Score one for fun chemicals secretly known to ogre spies.*

Kahg-Hahg quickly withdrew the parchment before Selene could get a whiff.

"Explain yourself!" Selene hissed.

"Forgive me, my Queen. Queen Najika of the Black Kingdom has a proposal for your ears only," Kahg-Hahg replied. "It is my judgment that she can be trusted."

I opened my mouth and prepared to speak as if my life depended on it.

It took a while. Too long, actually. It was cool in the great hall, but suddenly a sweltering heat seemed to have progressed from my face down to my waist. My sweaty palms showed the panic in my nerves, and by the time I completed my offer I could tell that I'd left Selene a lot to chew on.

Selene glanced furtively at the lolling head beside her, but Agtha didn't stir.

"This has never happened. Heads may disagree, but an ogre never contemplates killing his or her other self. It would seem too wrong. The others would never follow me if I committed such a crime."

"Then don't. Let me do it." I told her what I needed her to do, and to my relief she considered the radical thought…then considered what she had to gain. When she came to the conclusion I'd hoped for I nearly pumped my fist in the air and shouted.

"So, little Najika. Prepare yourself. We will meet in the arena." Selene turned to Kahg-Hahg. "Will you fetch us some water? Explain to Agtha when she wakes that your Queen was terribly dehydrated. It is a good thing you wetted our faces and revived us, isn't it?" Selene continued, her voice as suggestive as they came.

Chapter 20

Less than an hour later I realized one simple thing. Ogres had anger management problems. The arena was essentially a bare dirt field surrounded by roughly carved seats of stone. Ogres munched or chewed on giant haunches of meat, some cooked, some not. What made it harder to stomach was that their faces looked so human, each and every pair of them. I tried to ignore the tightness in my stomach, probably its way of screaming *Why are you about to get us both killed!?*.

Across from me stood a woman who could probably break mountains, or at least make a good dent in one.

Agtha-Selene wore plated steel armor, an ogre specialty. There were no easy gaps which my sword could exploit with a killing thrust. Only the ogre Queen's two heads were bare, as dictated by tradition. Even that wasn't much of a target though. Agtha-Selene hefted a shield made out of a gigantic reptile's skull. It was taller than me and wider than me, and it certainly looked a lot scarier than me.

"Why do I get the feeling that your Queen could flick me across the battleground with her index finger?" I grumbled. Kahg-Hahg knelt in the shadows just within earshot.

"Probably because she can."

As I walked out onto the field ogres jeered at me from all directions. It made sense for them to favor their own, and I didn't bear them any malice. They had no idea what I was really doing here anyway. I tried to focus, phasing out anything except the rictus of bloodlust on Agtha's face. She carried a mammoth's idea of a battle-axe. Just the axe's head weighed more than me and my horse would have combined.

I was on foot equipped with only a sword, my belt of throwing knives, and the war axe strapped to my back. Not exactly children's toys, but I had the reach of a child compared to the foe who now approached me like Goliath with me as the female version of David.

"Surrender now and I will make sure your death is swift!" Agtha called to me.

"Surrender now and I promise not to embarrass you in front of all your people!" I called back. I figured the angrier I could make her, the more likely she might make a mistake. Selene and I had to make this look convincing. If we didn't, if the ogres suspected what was really going on, then we were both dead.

A ring of ogre spears encircled the battleground, each thrust into the earth jagged point down. Traditionally the combatants would first walk in a circle and hurl them at each another while yelling creative insults. It was sort of the appetizer before the main course. The bad news for me, though, was that these spears were of ogre make, which meant they weren't designed to be lifted by humans. They weighed several times what I could even budge.

To say that 'battle was joined' was a generous way of putting it. Agtha-Selene put down her axe and hefted the first spear. I dodged as the long projectile tore a deep furrow in the earth where I'd just stood. The deadly barrage began. Agtha-Selene threw one murderous spear after the next. I ran, zigzagged, and fled for my life as the spears rained down on me. I was wearing my lighter leather breastplate, no chainmail. Agility was the one advantage I had over my lumbering opponent, and I planned to use it.

Another spear sailed my way, creating a buffet of wind that skimmed my face as I barely dodged what would have severed my head or at least left my face unrecognizable. Soon a thirteenth spear gouged the battlefield as I slid right, skidding at the last moment to reverse course, narrowly avoiding spear number fourteen just as spear number fifteen embedded in the ground in the same direction I had just turned to run.

I ran right into it, and the shaft of the spear made me see stars. I blinked, watching my vision swim as I dragged my feet forward, anything to keep moving. I heard a roar of laughter from the stands as the ogres enjoyed the sport. I heard rather than saw the latest hiss of air parting for the latest long pointy object of death. It missed my head by the width of a sparrow's wing. I felt its wind push me downward as I fell flat to the earth. Headfirst of course.

The ogre Queen had used only half of the spears encircling our battleground. At this rate I wouldn't even survive to the main event. It was time for a change in strategy.

The next spear seeking to puncture me went deep. Far too deep. That was because I was no longer dodging. I was advancing on the enemy. My throwing knives sang through the air, tiny whispers of death that bit into the soft flesh of Agtha-Selene's two faces. I made it look convincing, but a keen observer would have noticed that the knives thrown at Agtha's head seemed deadly aimed while the knives near Selene's face went wide.

Agtha shouted in fury as one of my throwing knives implanted in her neck. A trickle of blood started flowing down and underneath her plated armor, and I smiled just to see if it would infuriate her more. It did.

Now Agtha pulled her shared body with Selene towards the battle-axe, and Selene gave her control. Scooping it up in her enormous hands, the ogre Queen rushed me with a howl of fury coming from both mouths. Only one was genuine. I stood, waiting for the moment I hoped would come. Needed to come. The 600 pounds of muscular, feminine death bore down on me like a cliff face torn loose by an earthquake.

In the heartbeat before she was on me, Selene made her move. I looked down at the ogre Queen's feet and saw them stutter on purpose. She tripped forward and fell, sliding into a heap at my feet. I leapt, drawing my war axe. The sword wouldn't do. I needed something that could reliably hew through extra thick bone. I swung it in a vicious arc, and as Agtha raised her head my eyes looked into that face of bottomless hate. Then the moment was gone, and the head of my axe was cleaving through Agtha's skull. With a sickening crunch I felt it pierce…well, probably anything important.

My hands numbly gripped the axe embedded in Agtha's skull as Selene took control of her body and backhanded me. I flew several feet, but all she'd done was stun me. This too was part of the plan, though definitely not my favorite part. She sprang up with surprising athleticism for someone wearing heavily plated armor. Pounding the earth with her plated boots, she was on me too soon, looming like a shadow with the words *Die, puny human!* very much implied.

I'd just recovered feeling in my arms and legs when Selene grasped me by my ankles and lifted me up, dangling me like a worm. My vision swam and my face felt hotter than the sun, coated as it was in a thick layer of sweat.

"I surrender!" I croaked. The ogres roared in dismay. Some stood and shook their fists.

Until *she* spoke. "Sit your arses down and give me silence!" Selene roared.

The arena fell silent. You could have heard an ant climbing a pebble. I closed my eyes, hoping fervently that Selene wasn't about to double-cross me and brain me with her axe. Slowly, gently even, she lowered me to the ground. Made sure I didn't break my spine.

I sat up, panting heavily, every muscle screaming with pain about the unfairness of life. But I was alive.

"I accept your surrender, Najika. This fight is *done*." She turned to the other ogres, glaring at the audience until everyone found the clouds in the sky terribly intriguing.

Then she turned to me. "Don't think this makes us best of friends, Najika of the Black Kingdom. You owe me a treaty, and a fair one at that. We negotiate its major points *before* we agree to fight at your side, and not before."

I nodded, taking her hand as she offered it to me. But I couldn't lie to her. "You know I don't have complete authority. My husband can veto."

Selene gave me a disgusted look. "Yes, I know. You humans are so peculiar. Why do you even bother with husbands? They are only good for breeding and fighting."

I didn't respond to that, but my cheeks went hot.

Just then an ogre ran lumbering into the arena.

"Mighty Queen of All, there are humans approaching."

"Humans?" Queen Selene turned and looked at me. "Keep them waiting while Najika and I hammer out the key points of our new treaty. Also send for the amputation doctor. Tell Crorg that I need Agtha honorably removed and her head prepared for burial." She turned to me, her voice audible only to the two of us. "I have a treaty to make and dead weight to remove before we go greet these friends of yours. Come, we have a busy afternoon ahead of us."

Chapter 21

Imagine the biggest expression of shock you've ever seen. Now multiply that by a thousand faces and then some, and you have an idea of what we were about to create. My legs were burning. Every muscle was on fire. Nightfall enshrouded the world in its comforting moon-tinged blanket, and we were overlooking the valley of the Black Kingdom. The background noise of hundreds of ogres preparing their siege engines under cover of forest and darkness rolled through the trees in one constant, bustling susurration.

It had only taken an all-day march and then more plodding straight through dusk, hardly a break to be had. But now, like in any military operation, the old saying was true. It was time to 'Hurry up and wait.' All I could do was sit here as the ogre engineers made their preparations. I felt useless. Worse than useless.

"You look nervous. Queens don't have that luxury," Selene said.

"To be nervous?"

"No, to *look* so. I can tell you're new at this. Watch me. You might learn something."

I wanted to roll my eyes at the Queen of the ogres, but I wasn't sure that Queen Selene would take it with the good humor in which I intended it. Sometimes keeping something to oneself was the best move.

"Will they be ready in time?"

"Asking me that question twice already hasn't changed the answer, Najika, and I haven't learned anything new in the last hour. Be patient. Use this time to plan what you will do if we win. If that doesn't work, empty your mind. Focus on the sounds of the night."

I let out a frustrated sigh. "That doesn't help. It just makes me more aware of the engineers doing their work. Do you have any suggestions that will actually help?"

I risked a glance at the Queen of the ogres to see how well she'd taken my sarcastic tone. I hadn't meant to snap at her like that, but sleep deprivation can make tatters out of even the best intentions.

The Queen looked at me, and luckily I saw humor dance in her eyes. "You look like a stone rolled over you, Najika. Get some rest. Fighting on a few hours' sleep is better than none."

But I stubbornly shook my head no, and I had good reason to. When we'd entered the valley, Selene had sent Kahg-Hahg ahead to scout the area and make contact with the Black Knight's forces. The news had been grim and hopeful at the same time. The combined armies of the other Knights were assembled at the far end of the valley. To everyone's shock, though, rather than holing up in his stronghold to force a siege and buy the ogres some time to come relieve him, Drake had decided for the bolder move.

He'd moved his hopelessly outnumbered army onto the plains in front of the castle and deployed them for battle. Drake's allies, the trolls and the ape-men, were covering his flanks and had taken command of the high ground.

It still wasn't enough, but it had taken the enemy by surprise and forced them to delay while they redeployed their forces. Still, the result would be the same, Drake and his army defeated. Dying gloriously, perhaps, but dying gloriously all the same. When I finally got my hands on my husband I was going to throttle him. It took a special kind of nerve and stupidity to throw away an entire army.

An owl abruptly hooted through the night. Except it wasn't an owl. Queen Selene cocked her head, listening intently. Some of her ogre bodyguards rushed ahead, making similar sounds disguised as bird calls. I gave her a questioning look, and at last Queen Selene let me in on the secret.

"Those signals are my scouts' way of telling me that friends are approaching. Someone from your husband's army, I would guess. Soon we will see exactly where we stand."

If I was nervous before, my entire body now hummed with frayed alertness. I was exhausted, but my senses were heightened with anticipation. I was like a sleep-deprived dog on the hunt, and as long as the scent tormented my nose I had no choice but to move forward. I was glad that Lady Vaela and the still healing Bronwyn were safe back at the ogre settlement. If they could see me now...

My eyes made out three shapes moving in the darkness. Queen Selene and I stepped into the clearing, blinking as the moonlight washed over us and the newcomers came into view. My heart leapt and performed a victory whirl as I saw Drake in full battle armor striding through the knee-high grass. Two hulking shapes shielded him on both sides. One was more squat, the other taller and lithe.

I threw myself into Drake's arms. Or did he throw his arms around me? I didn't have the clarity to know which at this point. All I knew was that big, bulky arms were enfolding me and his nose was nuzzling my neck and cheek.

"It's good to see you," he whispered huskily. "You gave me a few scares out there." I assumed he was referring to my close brush with the Dreamgiver in the Rotted Wood and my fight to the death with Queen Agtha. He couldn't exactly toss blame about and cry foul, though. The idiot had jeopardized his entire Kingdom by using his black dragon to rescue me, and now he was risking his army when he didn't have to!

I stood back and gave him the most furious look I could muster while still being overjoyed to see him in one piece. Not an easy balance to strike.

"Why are you facing them in open battle!? You should be with your knights in the castle." I meant to whisper, but it came out more as a hiss.

"If I did that, Naji, then I would have one of two choices. I could either burn all the crops and houses outside of the castle, destroying my people's livelihoods to deprive my enemy of the resources…Or I could leave them like ripe fruit to be plucked, and the enemy would then use those supplies to outlast us as they besieged us into submission. Neither of those sounded attractive to me. If there's going to be a risk, it should be mine to take. My people shouldn't suffer while I sit back in my castle safe and sound."

"A noble speech, Black Knight, but I think Queen Najika is on the verge of slapping you. You might want to quit while you're ahead," Queen Selene said.

"You must be Queen Selene," Drake said with a bow, taking one of Selene's not-so-dainty hands and bringing it to his lips.

The Queen's eyebrow quirked, clearly intrigued. "And you must be the charming lord of the Black Kingdom. Your manners are better than I expected. Sometimes I forget that human males, unlike our own, have at least *some* capacity for refinement." Selene's obviously anti-male prejudice didn't seem to faze Drake.

He merely nodded.

"Zulz be thinking refinement is overrated," the tall figure on Drake's right rumbled. The one who seemed to call himself 'Zulz' in the third person looked familiar to me. He was enshrouded with wraps, folds of fabric disappearing over each other in a cloth-based maze which looped lovingly around his muscular torso. Then it hit me. He was a *troll*. One of the same people who had fought alongside me and Drake against the Red Queen.

Everyone gaped, even Queen Selene, when the tall troll removed his mask to introduce himself. Two long, gaping furrows tore canyons through his face, and what passed for a nose looked more like the snout of a feral beast. To call him hideous would have been honest, and it was also why trolls usually wore their masks. On coming of age, a troll's tusks were forcibly removed, leaving them scarred for life. Leaving the tusks in meant premature death as the tusks kept growing and curled inward, piercing the skull. Not a fun way to die.

Zulz gave Selene a challenging glare. "Zulz wouldn't mind an ogre female pitting her refinement against troll mettle any day. A battle of wills, yours against mine…you name the place, and Zulz be *there*." The troll chief somehow made those suggestive words both a challenge and an invitation. Queen Selene's eyes sparkled in reply as if she was deciding which. I'd never seen two creatures so repelled and attracted to one another simultaneously.

Drake tried to recover and take back control of the situation. I was fast learning that the more species of creatures you threw together, the more explosive things became.

"Queen Selene, this is the Chief of the trolls, Zulz. You'll have to excuse him. He's a bit deranged, even for a troll." At those words my husband shot Zulz a warning glare.

Then he turned to his left, where a squat figure covered in reddish-brown fur had eyes as big as my palms.

"This is Sebda, clan spokesman for the Ape-men." Sebda twirled about, somersaulting as his feet made circular motions in what seemed to signify some kind of 'hello.' His toes were every bit as flexible as my fingers, and they seemed to wiggle out their own special language in the brief time between when Sebda twirled and landed back on his feet.

"I greet you, Queen of the ogres." Sebda's human-like face smiled sadly. "Maybe next time I greet you death won't be hovering so near. One can hope, yes?" The ape-man had a strange cadence to his speech. Sometimes he sounded human, but at other times his voice rumbled almost like thunder.

"Zulz, Sebda, this is my wife and Queen, the Lady Najika," Drake said. I smiled as both troll and ape-man each took one of my hands, imitating my husband's bow as they kissed the backs of them. The rough texture of their lips felt like bark on my skin.

"Now enough with the introductions," Drake finished impatiently. "Let's get to it, shall we?"

Queen Selene nodded. "Let's. We will soon be ready for the attack."

Surrounded by the sighing trees that seemed to lament what would come, we made our final preparations for war. Dawn would be just another day for the birds chirping in the trees, but for us it meant something else. I told myself that I had a Kingdom to save even though I almost didn't believe it. Too much had happened in the last year. This would be my second real battle, and I still wasn't ready.

Chapter 22

The morning began with the twittering of birdsong nicely enough, followed by the lurch of catapults and loud echoes across the valley as huge, fiery stones whooshed through air. It was bizarre how death and harmony could mingle so closely side by side.

Drake's spearmen were in formation and advancing, his heavy cavalry of knights threatening to outflank the enemy or bolster the main line of attack. I rode beside Drake in the center of all that cavalry, my new ogre-crafted armor feeling like a second skin. Armor shouldn't feel as comfortable as satin, but somehow this suit did. I slid a look at Drake, who was watching the scene unfold dispassionately on the outside. I could sense the turmoil and fear underneath the mask he put up for his men.

"It should be interesting to see how the enemy responds to the ogre surprise," Drake said wryly. I looked up, watching as the enormous boulders rained from the sky, landing like colossal hailstones among the enemy knights. Soon the banners of each color—Gold, Green, Silver, Purple, and many others, all tried to reform and lead a two-pronged assault, one into the woods to strike at the source of those hurling boulders and another to charge the Black Knight's army.

But as the enemy knights formed up in good order, and despite watching some of their fellows smashed into pulp by the falling stones, a solid wall of ogres appeared at the tree line and began to descend along the northern slope.

There were many intimidating things about an ogre's size, and being a few heads taller than any human was definitely a big part of it. But what made it far worse was their strength, and the solid plated armor which made them look twice as massive as they really were. I imagined the looks on all the enemy knights' faces as this solid formation began to advance on them. I imagined the fear creeping into the enemy knights as that wall drew closer and the ogre figures became larger and more distinct.

The first charge of the enemy cavalry came from the ranks where the fluttering banners proclaimed the colors of the Yellow Knight and the Brown Knight. Drake and I watched as the warhorses churned their way up the slope. The knights looked formidable, especially with their lances leveled and ready to skewer anything in their way. Yet the ogres were not easy prey, and they had a nasty surprise—war hammers the height of a man's torso, each hidden and strapped behind the back. A solid swing with a war hammer could not only unhorse a knight, it could also cripple the horse.

And this is what we saw on a frightening scale. In a well-timed burst of violence the front line of the ogres released their war hammers and swung. Knights and warhorses crashed to the earth, but the knights were too disciplined to be so easily beaten. Many managed to get through the first rank of ogres, their lances finding a vulnerable spot in an ogre's helmet or piercing a rare weak point in the armor.

With mounting concern I saw the knights punch gaps in the ogre wall before drawing their swords and maces. More columns of knights crashed through, tunneling deeper into the ogres like antlered earthworms as they hacked and butchered their way forward. In close combat with the knights who'd already breached the front lines, the ogres didn't have the maneuvering space to swing their hammers. Still, the war hammers were more than just weapons of brute force. The head of each hammer had a long spike perfect for precise thrusts. The ogres began to systematically impale any knights who had managed to push beyond the first line of defense.

Soon it dawned on me what I was really seeing—the overconfident wave of attacking knights being incrementally shredded into ever finer pieces as their formations splintered and dug horns into the more resilient ogre forces. The losses on both sides were still sickening. I watched as one knight managed to cleave his way through an ogre's defenses, blood spurting to block both combatants from view. When the blood splattering was over the knight raised a sword no longer shining but now covered in gore.

"Shield up!" Drake shouted. I put up my shield just in time as arrows veered for my face. I felt barbed arrowheads beat harmlessly against my armor, but my heart lurched at the idea that my horse might not have been as lucky.

"They have archers in the trees. Stay sharp!" Drake said to me. I'd become so caught up in the main fighting that I'd forgotten that this entire area was still a battlefield. Death was never far. I sensed a turning of the tide, though, and as I peeked my head over the lip of my shield I saw the ogre horde beginning to grind away at the horns of each knight formation.

Meanwhile the ogre catapults continued to launch their deadly rain. Men and horses screamed in the most awful mix of sound. Of all the parts of battle I hated, the *sounds* of battle were high up on my list. My eyes began to search for the banner of the White Kingdom among the multitudes of enemy troops. *Father, are you out there?* Had an ogre boulder crushed him already? As if it hadn't been gripping me already, dread now swirled around me like a snake around the neck.

Then I heard what might as well have been the most beautiful music. I heard the call of a horn to signal retreat, and then I saw the forces of the other Kingdoms withdraw in good order. They kept withdrawing until they were well out of range of the ogre siege engines. A stillness settled over the battlefield of broken men and horses. Butchered ogres also littered the edge of the field. Other than the groans of the wounded and dying there was little to hear. The spearmen of Drake's army had been ordered to stop their advance, each man standing restless, probably wondering if he had a chance at cheating fate.

Then I saw him, a man on a horse with a white flag that the wind seemed to enjoy thrashing back and forth.

A herald, his boyish face confessing him to be hardly a man, trotted nearer. He was as skittish as a colt. The pale shade of his face admitted his fear. I would have laid bets on him wetting himself, but I wasn't the gambling type.

Drake and I exchanged looks, and together we rode out to meet him. Several of our knights covered our flanks, making sure this wasn't a trap.

When at last the herald reined in his horse, his beast pawed nervously at the ground and snorted.

"I come with tidings from the Knights of Arkor. They judge that perhaps this senseless bloodshed could be averted," the young man said carefully. "They request time to draw up a proposal for peace."

My husband snorted, but I was the one who replied. We'd already agreed what would happen if the enemy showed any openness to negotiating.

"Tell your leaders that we attack at midday unless they commit to a pact of non-aggression. It is too early to hope for a lasting peace," I warned, my voice as severe as I felt. "But we also do not desire bloodshed. No more need die today, or on any day after, in senseless violence. We will parley with your leaders tomorrow if they withdraw their forces from the valley and give us their oaths."

My flowery speech was typical of the custom of Arkor and even the Black Kingdom. Knights and their envoys were supposed to speak in noble terms, as if it could somehow sanitize the butchery of war. Yet I was disgusted by it, disgusted by the wasted humanity laid bare on a field that had been beautiful until this morning. I saw clusters of the dead clumped here and there on the plain like stands of weeds.

Vultures already circled in the cloudy sky.

After a long pause the young man nodded. "I will pass on your words to my Masters. You will have an answer before midday."

As the young man whirled about his mount and cantered back with a speed that comes only from fear, I reached out to squeeze my husband's hand.

"Do you think they'll see reason?" I asked.

Drake leaned over, his hands cupping my face as his lips gently caressed mine. "Let us hope, sweet Naji. Let us hope."

I was a little surprised at this public display of affection, but when I pointed it out Drake just cracked a gigantic smile.

"The enemy saw what I wanted them to see, Naji. A ruler so unconcerned with the outcome of the battle, so assured in victory, that he would lovingly kiss his Queen in the middle of a battlefield. Give me some credit. I do things for a reason."

I shot him a suspicious look. "If you say so…but I think you just wanted an excuse to kiss me." I tried to joke with him because it got my mind off of the nervous energy creating mayhem everywhere I could feel. Would the Knights accept our offer? Or would more blood be spilled?

Chapter 23

It had been four days since my agreement with Queen Selene. Four days since Lady Vaela found, to her amazement, that a lasting alliance with the ogres was reality.

It had been only a day since the bloody battle in the fields in front of Drake's castle, with frightening losses suffered on both sides. It was a battle which I thought could have gone on all day if the ogre siege engines hadn't brought the Knights of the other Kingdoms to their senses. I had done my part, and the part of me that wasn't knotted by nerves was actually swelling with a touch of a pride.

Today was more important than any day yet, and for good reason. It wasn't every day that you could avert a war.

On one side of the negotiating table on the greenway in front of the castle stood the Black Knight and his Queen—that's me, by the way—joined by the ogre Queen Selene and the leaders of the trolls and ape-men.

On the other side of the table stood the Knights from the Kingdoms of all the colors with the most clout—the Gold Knight, the Green Knight, the Silver Knight, and the Purple Knight, not to mention the Red Queen who now served as regent for her youngest son. But what made every nerve in my skin painfully alert was the sight of the White Knight, my father, standing at the head of the opposing delegation.

His stoic gaze roamed over my ornate battle-armor while studiously avoiding my face. The armor fitted snugly around my arms, chest, and legs, making me look beautiful and deadly. It was amazing what ogre armorers could smash together and custom-fit on short notice. The war axe I'd used to crack Agtha's head open like an egg was strapped firmly to my back for good luck, its wickedly sharp head peeking over my shoulder like a murderous wink. Okay, so I had to admit, it was mainly there as intimidating eye candy.

My father Kovinus put his quill to parchment and signed his name. Each of the other Knights at the table followed his lead, and finally Queen Agwen affixed her red seal, which was another acceptable symbol of agreement. She looked up at me as she drew away, and I knew that being foiled a second time would not stop her scheming mind from finding new and creative ways to plot my death.

After Drake, me, and our allies had also all signed the non-aggression pact, there was a strained shaking of hands. A very strained shaking of my hand with Queen Agwen's. The red-haired woman's fingernails scraped like claws, and I was glad for the gauntlets serving as a barrier between my skin and hers. Each second her cold eyes paid me attention was like another whisper saying *No,*

I haven't forgotten that you killed my son, and one day I'll mount your head over my fireplace.

But I wasn't about to give Agwen the satisfaction of unchallenged intimidation, even if she did do a mean stink eye.

"I hope that next time we meet under different circumstances," I said to her as our hands parted. "I wonder what things your son never got the chance to show me." Her lips curled as she bit back a snarling reply and then offered me the most pleasant smile.

"You would be most welcome to visit any time, Queen Najika."

"Oh, I have no doubt. But I can't promise that, when I *do*, I will be a very well-behaved guest," I replied, stroking the row of throwing knives at my waist. She took the hint. I saw a flicker of fear in her eyes as she turned away and fled.

Last of all I gripped my father's hand, but he shocked everyone there by firmly shaking my hand in return rather than moving briskly away.

"May I speak with you alone, Najika?" I nodded, automatically walking a good distance ahead of him, waiting until a cluster of trees obscured us from sight. I turned and prepared for things to get ugly. To be told that I was demon spawn leading an alliance of evil creatures, of ogres and trolls and things which hated humanity.

Instead I saw Kovinus take off his gauntlets, throw them to the ground. He reached one hand to my slender face, stroking my cheek.

I looked at him, confused. "This was one of the scariest days of my life," he whispered. "This could have been a day of bloodshed, the day I faced my daughter on the battlefield."

I finally saw a shred of emotion leak through his aging mask. I shuddered, my body going from hot to freezing, then back to scorching, emotion whiplashing across my heart. I bent my head down, tears stinging my face...but he just wiped them away. Wiped them away and said nothing else. I leaned into him, my head resting on the ivory cloth which curved over his shoulder. His arms gently enfolded me, holding me like I was a fragile thing instead of a woman bristling in combat armor.

Maybe he was worried he'd prick a finger on my axe, but I doubted it. His lips brushed my brow before he drew away. I wanted to call out to him. I wanted to tell him everything, how somehow things had turned out all right. How this was nothing like the life I would have had with the Red Knight. I wanted to tell him that I'd found happiness, crazy as it seemed.

But then I understood that this was as far as he would come. At least for now. And for him it was a mighty canyon leap just to show affection for his daughter and for once leave the question of duty aside. He had always been about duty, duty above everything. Even above those he loved. *Especially* then, as if to prove his moral worth. Yet as he walked away from me over the green field, I saw him glance back.

Maybe one day he would be ready for something more. Maybe it had taken actually losing me to realize what I meant to him.

I stood there watching him, so long lost in my own thoughts that I didn't notice Drake sneak up behind me. I jerked when he wrapped his armored arms around my waist. His head nuzzled my neck before he kissed the top of my head.

"A gold coin for your thoughts?" he asked.

"My thoughts aren't worth a copper bit," I replied, the bittersweet aftereffects of the encounter with my father still clinging to me.

"Now I doubt that," Drake whispered in my ear. "I seem to remember someone fitting your exact description coming out of the mountains at the head of an ogre army larger than anyone expected. Someone who did *that* must have some pretty useful thoughts," he argued.

I let him win me over, rewarding him with a reluctant smile. I turned in his arms, giving him a firm, full kiss. "Yes, well...I didn't want you to have all that fun without me. What would they have said?" I said mockingly. "The Black Knight vanquishes nearly a dozen armies with his wife nowhere to be found. Then you would have been insufferable."

"You mean I'm not already?"

I batted him on the nose. "Quiet. You were just becoming tolerable."

As we turned to walk side by side, I said the question that had been bothering me since the instant I'd returned from my mission to find Drake preparing for battle.

"Why didn't they keep fighting? They might have won, even with our siege engines."

My husband laughed. "*Might* have, sweet Naji. It's nice to know that there's a little naiveté left in you."

I tried to look hurt. I could do a mean pout when I wanted to.

"You're sleeping in the courtyard tonight."

His grin deepened. "I've been meaning to do some stargazing actually." It took him a few moments to turn serious. "No, Naji, I think that Queen Egwen had planned to crush us. With the ogres out of the fight, we wouldn't have had a chance. When they showed up in a big way, ready to fight for us thanks to you, it wasn't a gamble she was ready to commit to. According to my spies it was she, the Green Knight, and your father who were the three strongest advocates for peace. Of those three, I think only one had pure motivations."

I looked at him, and my heart did a celebratory flip. "Did I just hear you correctly?"

"Yes, Naji. You did. I think your father still loves you."

It was appalling how well Drake could read my emotions. I slipped my hand into his as we walked under the midday sun. The castle of the Black Kingdom loomed over us like an overprotective mother bear, and I knew one thing for sure. It was good to be home.

EPILOGUE

I lay naked but warm, the castle's chill not able to penetrate the heaping comforter or the campfire's worth of warmth coming from Drake's body. It had been nearly a month since the peace had been made, but now it was the eve before we were to attend court and officially thaw relations with the other Kingdoms. I couldn't sleep. The thought of seeing Father, not to mention former friends and allies who had abandoned me the moment I'd been disgraced…it just set my teeth on edge.

I didn't want to do this, but I also didn't want Drake to go alone. *Besides*, a small voice tugged at me, *this would be your first long adventure together.* Yes, perhaps if I just looked at it that way it wouldn't seem so overwhelming. The idea of meeting all the other Knights and their wives—and in some cases mistresses—didn't seem so much an adventure to me, though, as it did a tedious torture chamber. I was not a creature of politics. I was more at home eating in the kitchen with the castle servants, sharing questionable jokes over wine, rather than hobnobbing with royalty.

Although Father had tried to shield me from court intrigue as a girl, I remembered all the tensions. I remembered, when my mother was still alive, how she used to fidget and get easily upset with me the day before a court function. It seemed that any childhood memory I had connected with the court was also anchored to sadness. When my mother's heart failed her, maybe she had died peacefully as the court physician claimed.

But I doubted it, and secretly I resented the court politics which I blamed for devastating her nerves and inviting her to an early grave.

"Naji? What's wrong, can't you sleep?" Without even realizing it I'd crossed to the outer chamber beyond our bedroom, thrown open the drapes and looked out over the pensive night. Drake's warmth enfolded me from behind, but a chill still crept along my collar bone as if to remind me tomorrow would be here too soon.

I turned my head, kissing his hand where it rested just below my shoulder. "Not a wink," I said. "Too restless thinking about what's ahead, I guess."

His eyes softened as his hands started a gentle, stroking pattern along my shoulders and arms.

"You don't have to go, Naji. Staying here and looking after the Kingdom is more than understandable. You *are* the Queen after all. No one would think less of you for safeguarding our Kingdom in my absence."

I sighed. "No, Drake. Your mother can do a fine job here without us. If you think I'm made of steel, try taking a look at the diamond underneath her skin. I think even that savage troll king doesn't know what to make of her." I thought back to the celebration banquet where our motley group of allies had all sat and dined together after the non-aggression pact had been made. It had been a bizarre sight.

Drake chuckled. "I was just remembering my mother teaching Zulz to use eating utensils. Did you see the look on the troll's face when she threatened to stab him in the hand with her fork?"

"You mean when he tried to reach for that slice of ham?" I replied, giggling. "Yes. I don't think I've ever seen a creature that big scared of something so much smaller," I added.

We talked a little more by the window, and soon it became clear that he was just as restless as me.

"We're going to be useless tomorrow. You do know that?" Drake asked. I chuckled.

"Fair enough, but I can't control how I feel." I shrugged before letting out an exasperated sigh. "I think I'll take a walk. Some fresh air in the courtyard might help." I could tell that Drake was about to offer to join me, but I knew better than he did that a good sparring session unwound his nerves better than almost anything.

"Why don't you go wake Sir Stavros? I'm sure he would be up for a vigorous sparring session. It would be a great workout for you and get your mind off of things."

Drake cocked an eyebrow at me. "Are you trying to get rid of me? Because I warn you...after my sparring session I may still be restless, and you look beautiful tonight."

He deserved the tormenting he was about to get. I twirled in his grasp, giving him a tantalizing view obstructed by shadow. "Perhaps I'll be your captured princess later on. Now off with you. Shoo!"

I think Drake could tell that I needed to be alone with my own thoughts because he didn't argue. Smart men did that sort of thing. After he'd left I shrugged into my night robe and prowled the corridors overlooking the courtyard. The night was unexpectedly chilly with the whispery breeze. Something rumbled in the distance even though the charcoal sky seemed placid enough. There was this odd thrill to what I was doing, walking the castle corridors without servants to trip over, just having the whole fortress to myself.

At night the whole world seemed to vanish, and the lack of distractions sometimes brought out the thoughtful side in me. I continued down the winding marble staircase that led to the audience chamber and throne room. There was something hushed and holy about the place as I walked in. Its cavernous space seemed to hide mysteries.

"It's a beautiful night."

My body went ramrod straight. A chill, and not from the breeze coming through the open windows, stroked the length of my spine.

I said nothing. What did you say to someone who had accused you of horrible things? Lady Vaela sat on her chair in the throne room, idly turning a jar filled with fine dust over and over in her hands.

I recognized it all too well. When Drake had used the dragon on his great-sword, summoning it to save me from the Dreamgiver, his great-sword had turned to dust. The fine granules in that jar were all that remained. Ever since that day when Lady Vaela had accused me of forcing Drake to squander the Black Kingdom's most precious weapon, talk between us had been scarce. And by scarce, I meant nonexistent.

Somewhere I understood the pressures she'd been under. I mean, just thinking about it...two of her sons trying to have her eldest son and his new wife killed...that had to be a nightmare for her. What kind of internal conflict had to be raging in her heart? But that nagging voice in my head reminded me that she had thought my life wasn't worth saving. Drake using the dragon to save me was on the one hand this epic gesture of love that made my heart thump faster. Yet the not-so-girly part of me, the *You have a Kingdom to look after*, responsible side of me, told me that Vaela had been right.

"You scared me." What else was I going to say? What did you say when your mother-in-law sat like a ghost in a shadowy throne room at night and nearly terrified you out of your wits?

"Yes, well, I do have that effect on some people," she said, a tired note to her voice.

I walked briskly across the throne room, making a beeline for the exit. "Well don't let me disturb you," I replied.

As I walked past her, though, Lady Vaela got up from her throne, left the jar on the cushion and came over to me, snagging my wrist in a gentle grasp.

"Don't go, Najika."

"If it's all the same to you, I'd prefer to," I said, my stomach tightening. She'd noticed the way I'd flinched when she touched me. I saw her eyes widen as if she'd been struck.

"I see," Vaela said, her eyes going down to the floor. But then her gaze surged up, trying to capture mine. "Will you stay, then, if I beg you to?"

"I think I know your feelings well enough," I said with venom before I could control it. "You'd rather see me dead and your Kingdom safe. I think that spells things out pretty clearly. Don't you?" My eyes must have blazed, because she took a half step back as if I'd slapped her. Then she found her courage. My cheek stung as she *actually* slapped me. Hard.

"I love you like the daughter I never had!" she cried. "What I said was wrong, and if it hadn't been for you, the ogres would never have helped us. In the long term your survival is what has made my Kingdom safer, and not a day goes by that I don't regret what I said to you," she said, tears shining in her eyes.

"I was being small-minded, Najika. I was being selfish and small-minded and stupid. That's what happens when you assume that the end justifies the means without looking at the long term picture or what's inside your heart." She slumped, looking older and frailer than I had ever seen her.

"Now stop resenting me with all of your pent-up anger, Najika. Let it out. I deserve it. I deserve the slap I just gave you tenfold." She rose up, her bearing proud. "Go ahead. Give me what I deserve. Don't hold back."

The first time I slapped her it felt good. But not good-good. It was a guilty pleasure vindictiveness type of good that snuck through me as my hand connected with her cheek. Then, as if a mob of tiny angels had overpowered that gleeful, vengeful me, I crushed her with an *I haven't seen you in ages* hug we'd never shared before.

"I've been really angry with you," I whispered. I cursed myself as my eyes became a waterworks. I tried to sniff back the traitorous tears, but they were ruthless and charged down my face anyway.

I tried to talk through them. "And it's been that much harder because I admire you, Vaela, your strength. How devoted you are to your son." I probably kept babbling on, but my mind mercifully didn't remember anything I said after that. I felt Lady Vaela squeeze me back with a hug just as crushing. Then, when we finally pulled apart, our tear-ruined faces exchanged rueful looks.

"Your face is a little puffy. How's mine?"

"I'm afraid it's just as bad," I replied, and we both smiled.

"Then I guess we make a good match," Lady Vaela said. I looked back at the only other woman in the world who loved Drake as much as I did, and a major rift in my heart seemed to mend. If

Drake and I were about to embark on the most annoying journey of a lifetime, at least I was leaving things intact behind me. I was glad that we'd reconciled, as unlikely and as unusual as the reconciliation had come about.

"Would you take a walk with me in the courtyard? I was hoping you might give me some advice on how to handle the Knights and ladies at court," I said. "I'm not really looking forward to it." The truth was that I would rather dig knives under my nails and listen to myself scream, but sometimes it was best not to tell your mother-in-law everything.

Lady Vaela's eyes lit up like I'd just given her a room brimming with gold. "I would be delighted to." She took my hand, and as we turned to walk away I swore that I noticed the fine dust from Drake's great-sword shift in its jar, swirling into what looked almost like a miniature dragon, smoke curling from tiny nostrils as it schemed with a mind of its own. Then it was gone, sooner than the gap between one heartbeat and the next.

Weird. Sleep deprivation must have been turning my head into a puddle of mush. There were certainly enough other worries cluttering it. As Lady Vaela and I walked hand in hand into the cool privacy of the night, I still had to wonder. What would the future hold? Whatever the next adventure might be, at least I wouldn't be facing it alone.

End of Book One

Najika's story continues in *The Princess Who Tamed Demons*

Coming 2015

Acclaim for The Princess Who Defied Kings and the stories of J. Kirsch

"Excellent, powerful, vivid writing! [Fantasy and Science Fiction] just doesn't get any better than this!"

—*K. G. McAbee, fantasy author and winner of the Black Orchid Award*

"Good writing. Good characters."
—*Barnes&Noble Nook Book, User Reviews*

"Well-written."
—*Barnes&Noble Nook Book, User Reviews*

"Loved the characters."
—*Barnes&Noble Nook Book, User Reviews*

"Taut [and] engaging…"
—*J. A. Johnson, author of the Wild, Wild Quest Trilogy*

"Princess Naji is someone I would stand and fight beside any day of the week."

—*Goodreads Review*

"If you like adventure, fantasy with a little mystery…then this is your book."

—*Goodreads Review*

"It has all the best elements of a good fantasy."

—*Goodreads Review*

"Princess Najika has a strong, refreshing voice."

—*Goodreads Review*

Author's Note:

Thank you for reading this book. Please take a moment to rate it and share your thoughts on Smashwords, Goodreads, Barnes & Noble, Amazon or wherever you prefer! It's rewarding to hear from readers like you.

You are welcome to visit my website at **J. Kirsch Books** to take a peek at my upcoming novels and current projects. You can follow me on Twitter where I post under the nickname **librarian4smash**. To reach me by email send a message to: jkirschbooks@gmail.com. I always respond to queries and questions. Feel free to comment on my science fiction and fantasy blog, **Starfarers and Knights**.

Below you'll find *Part One* of my science fiction & fantasy book, **Crysalis: Vira's Tale**.

Welcome to the world of Crysalis...

In the distant future, the last remnants of humanity huddle in fragmented societies deep below ground, struggling to stay alive while threatened with inconceivable dangers. Three strong women from three different cultures are on intersecting paths, heading towards a fateful meeting which may well be mankind's only hope for survival...

Crysalis: Vira's Tale

J. Kirsch

Chapter 1

"We've been patient enough, Robles. I don't think you're going to be able to come up with what we need."

The slender man sat with one shadow poised across the table, and another hovering at his shoulder. Robles began to tremble. His assailants might have been wearing black-and-tan body-suits, typical uniforms for any citizen of Beta Sector, but the hard, focused intent in their eyes said that these were not ordinary working men.

"Please...I can pay back all of it and interest! I just need more time. Don't take my family!"

Damian Luxe smiled grimly. It had been an uneventful night at the Twin Galaxies until now. The young man cracked his head left and right, loosening up the muscles in his neck and shoulders. He stretched his arms, feeling the metallic exoskeleton hum as the joints slid along the well-oiled combat suit that hugged his body like a second skin. *Finally something with a little spice!* Damian thought.

He leapt over the nightclub's railing, landing right behind Dirt Bag Number One. The angry man cursed and reached for a six-inch blade concealed at his ankle. Damian's hand curled around the offender's wrist, snapping it like a wishbone.

"AAAGGHHH!!!" Dirt Bag Number Two drew out a sawed-off energy pulse cannon and pulled the trigger. Damian swore, diving for cover as he took Mr. Robles down hard alongside him, aware of the table blowing apart into shards and splinters.

The gun-toting killer stepped over the table's remains, poised to unload point-blank into Damian's chest when the bouncer's left leg cut the man's feet out from underneath. Damian leapt across, grappling for the weapon, but in all the struggling it flew clear. The killer's partner grasped the weapon with his remaining good hand and managed to steady it at Damian's head.

Damian had time to register disbelief. What kind of drugs was this guy taking that he could coolly block out the pain of a broken wrist? And how did that gun slip through entrance security? It shouldn't even have been possible. *Possible or not, I'm about to be just as dead.*

Damian's disbelief made a sharp turn, though, when a bottle of Lavaburst whiskey – so high in quality that its sacrifice really was a tragedy – broke over the assailant's head in a melee of flying fluid and glass. A young woman, not more than 19 or 20 stepped back and gaped in shock at what she'd done. The dirt bag she felled was unconscious, and blood began pooling around his head.

Damian didn't have time to thank her. He was busy pummeling the ribs and face of the other too-close-for-comfort assailant. Finally, satisfied that the man underneath him wouldn't so much as twitch, Damian stood up and turned to speak to his unlikely rescuer.

She was gone.

Three other bouncers meanwhile had just converged on the scene.

"Son of a—Luxe, you seeing stars, buddy?"

Damian Luxe shook his head free of any disorientation. "No, and no thanks to *you*, Jenson." Damian turned to glare at Kavrik and Gunther too. All three of his fellow bouncers wore the same B-grade exosuit that he did. Physically they were super-strong, but no amount of strength was any protection against an energy pulse that could make pulverized meat out of your internal organs.

"That looked pleasant," Kav said, palming the fallen weapon. "I'll take this to Yoji." Yoji would just about have an aneurism. He supervised the club's day to day affairs, and would have to report the incident to the Crew Authority. From there they would hopefully follow up to find out which crime syndicate these two pieces of space trash worked for.

But Damian couldn't get one image in particular out of his adrenaline-soaked brain.

She looked terrified, like the last person in the universe who would play hero, he thought. He remembered a small nose and gold-green eyes enshrouded in a mass of dark, shoulder-length hair. Whoever she was, he didn't seem to remember ever seeing her before, and that both frustrated and intrigued him. He always repaid a debt.

"Did you see the girl who smashed her whiskey bottle into that bug-head who was about to make spare parts out of me?" Damian asked.

Gunther and Jenson shrugged. "Sorry, brother, we had a little outbreak of drunken cat-fighting on the dance floor. We didn't see you were in trouble until the crap had already hit the skids and run its course."

Damian sighed, but he couldn't claim to be genuinely pissed. Nine out of ten times, it was the drunken partygoers on the dance floor or at the bar who got out of hand. It made sense that they'd been keeping a close eye there, and responding with overwhelming force. It was so seldom anything serious happened...you had to be stupid or very powerful to carry a weapon into a public place. The Haven's Crew Authority frowned on that...big time.

First offense was temporary detention and psych evaluation. Second offense rated you 'excess organic waste' to be recycled into the maintenance systems or dropped down some forgotten shaft.

A rustling movement caught his eye under the strobe light near the club's back exit, where Damian thought he saw a petite shape slip into the rearmost corridor of Sector G. Is that her? He burned on instinct and bolted for the swinging doors. Three seconds later he burst onto Starview Avenue, a corridor wide as a thoroughfare and teeming with throngs of colonists looking to get their entertainment fix.

Damian saw flashes of dark hair and the back of a head. Not much to go by, but instinct kept urging that there was something familiar to it. One thing that made Damian an effective bouncer was his keen memory for bodies and faces. Once a dumbass got banned from the club, he didn't sneak back in no matter what disguise he wore, not on Damian's watch.

The bouncer shoved his way through the crowd, aided by the exosuit which persuaded everyone to give way. Jenson wasn't far behind him, yelling that he was going to get himself in knee-deep excrement. He didn't have authorization to wear brawling gear outside of his work duties. All weapons in Beta Sector were strictly regulated.

They can bite me, he thought. If he didn't catch this girl now he doubted he'd ever see her again. It killed him that he'd been saved by her random act of courage, and he'd be damned if he didn't at least see the look on her face and offer to repay her for what she'd done.

He darted down two more corridors, flowing past well-lit storefronts and barreling through a moving 3D promo. An exquisitely beautiful woman turned to him, her holographic features shimmering as she spoke seduction.

"In Pick Your Own Reality, no adventure is beyond your grasp. Come. Come. The hero inside you beckons." She smiled, her arm flung wide to indicate the apartment complex where some people would spend a day's creds to live out entire lives in time-dilated artificial worlds. A girl ran inside as the glass doors yawned open, and now Damian was sure. It was definitely her.

Damian launched ahead with more haste than he'd intended. He hadn't intended to be moving so fast that he completely shattered the sliding doors before they could give way. Oops.

He turned left and right, feeling strange to finally be here. Friends and acquaintances had gushed about the place. Anorax's Alter-Reality was every bit as real as anything The Haven could offer...only more so. There you could feel a breeze tickle the skin of your cheek. Here you could feel recycled air.

The exosuit-buffed bouncer clearly intimidated the single employee on duty. He was young and pale-skinned, with a tall blade of hair marching down the middle of a shaved head and a tattoo running under his left eye.

"Yo, brain-dead, any particular reason you feel the need to trash a perfectly fine entrance? Those creds coming right out of your account, fool." Damian was impressed with the kid's bravado, but it didn't fool him for a moment. The bouncer cornered the kid behind his desk and thrust his strength-enhanced hands to both sides, making fist-sized dents in the cheap countertop.

"The girl who ran through here. Which way?"

"You've signed up for all kinds of crazy, haven't you? Just forget I said anything. She went that way." The young man pointed and made a desperate shooing gesture.

"Thanks." The apartment doors which Damian flitted past were probably locked, and he didn't want to barge into one random room after the next. But he was 99% sure that she hadn't gotten that far ahead of him. Unless she knew this place a hell of a lot better than he did, Damian thought he had a decent shot of catching up to her. He rounded another corridor. The black-painted walls and bluish lighting made it hard to see, and abruptly someone's legs were dropping right on top of him. Those same powerful legs rested on his shoulders and he felt a sharp object being thrust between the joints of his exosuit, ready to prick an artery.

"So much as breathe funny and I will gut you," said a feminine voice.

Not half bad. Damian froze. "Listen, I'm not here to hurt you. I actually wanted to thank you."

"For what?"

"For saving my life. Of course it's kind of ironic since you have a blade to my throat now. Maybe we could take the irony down a notch. How about you slowly remove that knife and get off of me, and we talk like two normal people?"

"I didn't ask for your gratitude or your—"

"Damian. Please call me Damian. Do you have a name too, or should I just call you 'Knife-girl'. Not that it doesn't have a nice ring to it, but—"

"What do you want? Tell me that much and maybe I can see things your way," she replied.

"You saved my life back there, and I want to know why."

"You were just doing your job. Those scum rats deserved what they got. I was just at the right place, at the right time. There's no big mystery, Damian. Just go back to your life, and let me go back to mine."

As she said it, the dark-haired girl slowly leapt backward. Graceful as an acrobat, she landed on her feet and carefully backed away. But Damian had already whirled and taken note of her disheveled looks. Her eyes appeared haunted...every bit as tired as they were fierce. She had bathed recently, which was good. The homeless didn't last long in Beta Sector. The android guards did regular sweeps to clean out the human dregs, and scent was their simplest and easiest criterion to categorize someone as—and it didn't exactly flow off the tongue- 'excess organic material.'

The girl's jacket was torn, though, and her body-suit pants were worn in at least half a dozen scrapes. A deep gash across her left shoulder told Damian that she'd probably collided with something inconvenient in her rush to flee the scene at the club. He noticed too, for the first time, how beautiful her face was, how her deeply bronzed skin set off the color of her eyes and a cute nose with very kissable lips.

Damn it, Damian. Keep it in your pants. Don't be an ass. He noticed ruefully that the grime on her face looked like it had been accumulating, and this wasn't normal. Citizens were anal about hygiene. It would take one plague or virus to decimate entire sub-sectors and turn Beta Sector into a giant kill zone. From birth, children were indoctrinated in cleanliness, cleanliness, cleanliness. There was only one reason that a person would look the way she looked...

"You need a place to stay?"

"Me? No thanks. You hard of hearing, Damian? I said—"

"I heard what you said," Damian grunted. He licked his lips and tried to act natural. How did you act natural around a homeless girl whose very existence was illegal? He could turn her in for a small fortune. Never have to work another day in his life.

"Is that a 'No I don't need a place to stay' or a 'No I don't trust you farther than I can throw you?'" Damian asked.

The girl brushed an unruly tendril of hair out of the way, her other hand fidgeting with the knife. She stared at him oddly. She seemed to be sizing him up, but it was more than that.

"And if I did need a place to lick my wounds, what of it?"

"Look...far be it from me to ask you about your business," Damian tried. Careful, dumbass. Don't spook her! "I could just give you the key-print to my place. I can stay with a friend. No harm, no foul. You don't even have to see me again. Just stay a couple days…stay the week if you need to. Come by the club and leave me a note when you're ready to move on. Is that simple enough?"

"And just why would you do this for me?"

"What part of 'You saved my sorry ass back there, and I always help those who help me' seems so unbelievable to you?" Damian replied, sighing as he clenched his fists and wanted to say a few more things about hard-headed members of a certain gender.

The girl fidgeted with the knife again. She bit her lip as every muscle tensed. Seconds ticked by, too damn many, until her body relaxed. She returned the knife to the hidden sheath underneath her jacket and put both hands on hips.

"Slide me the key-print. Then turn around, go back the way you came. Tell your friends at the club that you weren't able to catch me. Deal?"

Damian nodded, suppressing the urge to grin like an idiot. It felt good to be doing her a kindness, repaying the debt. So why was his pulse tap-dancing? Why did it feel like he'd won the lottery to join the elites in Crew Sector? The young bouncer wasn't sure, but his subconscious seemed to know something the rest of his body didn't.

This won't be the last time we'll meet.

Chapter 2

Somewhere in Beta Sector an apartment hummed to life as Damian and Jenson awoke to the gentle, cascading whoosh of a waterfall.

"This is your new alarm, seriously? Absolutely. Pathetically. Lame." Damian groaned himself awake, but Jenson didn't even flinch.

"Really? You're going to fault a guy for having originality in his tastes and changing it up? Don't be a hater, dude. Shut up and make us some breakfast. If you're going to be a guest, at least make yourself a useful one."

Jenson padded bare-chested and barefoot through the bedroom to the stand-up shower stall, closing its glass door behind him. It fogged up almost immediately as steam hugged the ceiling. Damian heard a sigh of contentment from his co-worker as the water sprayed for all of 60 seconds – half of what the water system would allow during any 24-hour period.

As Damian brushed his teeth in the sink which was wedged tightly between the shower stall and the wall, his mind wandered. It had been one week since his agreement with the mystery girl. Through sheer force of will he had kept away from his own apartment, letting her stay at his place to the point where he had nearly worn out his welcome at Jenson's.

Jenson could be an ass, but he had Damian's back. They'd fought their way out of their share of scuffles in the past year at the club. Prevented more than a few concussions that way. Twin Galaxies attracted its share of scum and other types for whom scum seemed a generous compliment, and it didn't help that the club's owner was a major underworld figure. But the upside of it was that the bouncers were like a brotherhood. Often they carried themselves more like an elite security force than the young, testosterone-filled bruisers they were underneath.

"Look, my friend, I get that you have an eye for Mystery Girl. But is simply giving her the key-print to your apartment really the way to show it? That girl has one word written all over her, and it starts with a capital T."

Damian slammed his hand on the stall's surface. "None of that. I already violated her trust by telling you about her. You could at least be a little charitable."

Jenson stepped out of the shower, toweling off before putting on his gray-black body-suit. "You're misunderstanding. That's my whole point. The girl needs help, not another handout. If you check up on her, she'll know you actually care. And if you do it sooner rather than later, you'll actually have a chance in hell that she'll still be there, and that you can do something to help her before she gets herself killed."

Damian threw some biotech-improved bread slices in the toaster and turned on the coffeemaker on top of the fake marble counter. He drummed his fingers impatiently. "So...let me see if I understand you. You think she's Trouble, but that I should be like a moth heading towards the flame?" He didn't mention the other objection which loomed like a 900-pound mutant in the room.

The girl's an illegal. I can get exiled from the sector just for harboring her. More importantly, I could get a hefty reward for reporting her at the nearest Bot Station. So why haven't I?

Jenson was his friend, but Jenson was also a total sap. It made sense for the romantic pea-brain to think Damian could somehow save the girl. But what could he realistically do? It was easy enough to visit a lower sector, but all of the sectors underneath Beta were vicious. And Alpha? That was like praying for rain in a tunnel. Which left one option.

"I haven't exactly been reciting poetry, Jenson. I've been doing some research."

Jenson leaned on the counter beside him, swiping two mugs and pouring two helpings with a grace that disgusted Damian this early in the morning.

"Damian, I've been patient. I know you've been going 'out' each morning after work. Have I said a peep about it? No. But now I'm getting impatient. So spill...what so-called research?"

When Damian sullenly took a sip of coffee and refused to meet his friend's gaze, Jenson bumped him in the shoulder. "Fine, I'll sweeten the pot. I have a secret of my own, and it's pretty heavy. You tell me your secret, I *show* you mine."

Damian inhaled the toast, barely tasting it in the midst of this intriguing development. Could this be the same "Always-By-The-Book Jenson" that everyone at the club relentlessly teased? If Jenson had secrets, then two-headed mutants were sexy love magnets. Secrets?? The hell he did.

But Damian found himself humoring his good friend. He shrugged. "All right, you want in…fine. I've done a little digging on what it would take to get her fake identity papers to live in Beta."

Jenson's eyes widened. "Dude, people in that line of work lead only one kind of life, and they tend to be three things: ugly, brutish, and short. You'd have to go at least…*at least* Inner Fringe Sector for that stuff. The syn bosses will send their guys to Beta to put the heat on someone, but they don't do business here in Beta Sector. You know that. You're more likely to get yourself killed than to actually meet anyone down there who's acting in good faith!" Jenson was almost shouting.

The criminal syndicates could rot for all Damian cared. He still owed this girl a debt and there was something more to it, though Damian didn't feel like examining his own motivations too deeply. He felt what he felt, reasonableness be damned.

"You'd be surprised what an enterprising, curious person can find out with a little persistence."

Jenson groaned. "Have you been talking to those gen-freaks again?"

"The proper term is 'genetic freak' or 'alt,' and the answer is yes," Damian growled. "They've already given me directions to a place where we can do the swap. They've even made an approach on my behalf. I've proven that I can pay. All I need to do now is give them the signal."

Jenson sighed, rubbing the stubble on his chin. "I'm listening."

After Damian outlined his plan, Jenson nodded in all the right places, but he sighed twice as often. At last Jenson ran a hand over his buzzed hair and shook his head. "You're lucky that I'm almost as crazy as you are. I'll go with you, on one condition. Get cleaned up first...then I'll show you my secret."

Damian hopped in the shower for his 60 seconds, scrubbing ruthlessly with shampoo and soap before toweling off in record time. He shrugged into another gray-black body-suit as his friend wagged a 'come here' finger at him.

A minute or so later Damian's jaw had dropped away. *So much for the friend I thought I knew.* Damian was looking at a long folded-out work table that Jenson had hastily erected in the living area. It opened onto the adjoining kitchen, completing the second half of the apartment next to the bedroom. Damian's friend had pulled from the kitchen pantry not food...but two full exosuits. They looked horrendous. The metallic overlays had been bashed and dented into oblivion, then retrofitted and resurfaced.

"What the..." Damian honestly didn't know what to say.

"I'd like you to meet 'Vuldemort' and 'Dumbledoor.'"

"Where'd you come up with names like *that*?"

"They were noble politicians back on Earth. I heard a couple of guys at the club talking about them. Anyway...pay attention." Damian knew that most of the history of Earth was just a memory, or a memory of a memory of memory, but he didn't bother trying to correct his friend.

The two exosuits were about the same size, but examining Vuldemort more closely, Damian saw a tiny pinprick which shimmered on the underside of the breast-piece.

"Bleed me dry. Is this what I think it is?" Damian hissed.

"Yep, this baby's a reworked B-grade exosuit, courtesy of parts salvaged by yours truly. I can dumpster dive with the best of them. Oh, and yes, that blue sparkly is a force field converter crystal. Anything tries to invade your personal space, it's getting repelled in a major way."

"How did you get it?" Damian asked in awe.

Jenson chuckled. "Don't get too excited. A friend's neighbor passed away. You know how it goes...sometimes deaths take a while to get reported, and people on my friend's housing block tend to keep to themselves. He happened to mention it and I may or may not have used one of these B-grade retrofits to creatively 'open' the door. Knew I didn't have much time to take anything, so I nabbed the only really valuable thing I laid eyes on. It was tucked away between the cooker and the spice rack if you can believe it."

Damian wanted to swear, but instead he gave his close friend a stare of newfound respect. "I can't believe the same guy who won't shave the price of a single drink for a sexy girl in the club has the balls to break into an apartment and steal something worth more than our annual salaries combined. Who the heck are you?"

Jenson shrugged. "You have your hobbies, I have mine. The exosuits at the club have saved our lives countless times, but they'll never be ours. These babies are my pet projects. What else am I going to do, stuck in a system degrading faster than you can say 'garbage,' where the future is leading who the hell knows where?"

"When were you going to tell me about them?" Damian accused.

Now Jenson's smile grew beatific. "Vuldemort was going to be your big, nasty present when you hit your 20th. Guess what? We're celebrating your birthday early. Now here's my condition, as promised. We do this crazy, shady deal for your Mystery Girl only if you wear the suit. You wear Vuldemort. I'll go with Dumbledoor here, and besides, he'll do in a pinch as long as I don't take too many direct hits."

Damian nodded as he took one final gulp of coffee and stepped into his boots. He took one last scan of the Vuldemort suit with its pock-marked surface and cascades of dark streaks, alloy impurities left over from the mother of all repair jobs. It was a miracle the thing held in one piece, yet whoever had brute-forced the retrofit had known what they were doing. It looked sturdy as a rock.

"One last thing before you go flirt with your Mystery Girl and tell her the idiocy we're prepared to do for her," Jenson finished. "Keep in mind, my buddy who did the retrofitting and repair said that these suits aren't as stable as the certified 'Pure-B' exosuits manufactured in our Sector. In other words, this isn't your license to play hero."

"Got it."

"Number two, the sparkly on your exosuit has been degrading over time. My snooping didn't yield much useful info besides how to install them, but here's what I do know. Not even one of those crystals has been officially released from Alpha Sector in the last sixty plus years. That means this thing is probably old. How long its force field will last when triggered, that's a crap shoot if there ever was one. Could be an hour. Might be 10 seconds. Got it?"

Damian nodded. "Do you also plan to give me a tutorial on fire safety or can I go now?"

"Actually, there is one more thing."

"What?"

"Tell your Mystery Girl that if we get her those papers she owes me a kiss on the cheek."

Chapter 3

The young bouncer's veins thrummed with excitement, yet he was terrified. He didn't know if she was even still using his apartment. While he walked down Jefferson Avenue in the Archimedes sub-sector Damian wondered if he'd find that his apartment had been ransacked of everything valuable. *If she's desperate enough, she'll run. Who am I kidding? I would've probably done the same by now.* The Archimedes Sub-sector was as close as Beta Sector had to a downtown. As a single area carved out of rock, it towered at least a kilometer above its residents and was more than ten times that in width. He approached his apartment block, which was crisscrossed with wire mesh walkways whose ramps zigzagged before dropping to street level. Lights spilled underneath more doorways than not, many of them illuminating the etchings along every hall. The spans between many apartment doors were scrawled with the words and images of poets, madmen, hedonists, and every other malcontent who could suck in air. It was easier than trying to put anything useful up on the heavily censored community message boards.

If she's already scattered to the four directions, then this has all been one huge waste of time. He could always hope to track her down again, but in Beta Sector alone, with tens of thousands of people, was that anything more than a pipe dream?

He readjusted the strap on his shoulder. The canvas bag he hugged to his torso had a few things he hoped Mystery Girl would find useful. Despite the darkness under the door, he knocked. Waited. No sign. No motion. He waited some more. Knocked again, softer this time.

It was late morning. The girl probably stayed put during the day. Less risk that way. He might have woken her. He had to hope that was why she hadn't opened the door yet, especially since he didn't like some of the alternatives.

"Look…hey, it's me. I need to come in. I've brought you some things. Try not to knife me in the face, okay?" No answer. He pressed his face up against the door, and a screen shimmered over the door's surface. The door doubled as a retina scanner for ID purposes in case a resident lost their key-print and hadn't yet been able to replace it. The door clicked, unlocking, and Damian stepped through.

The lights had been dark, but they immediately turned on as they sensed Damian's movement. Not so with the bedroom. The light settings here were different, for the usual reasons. Damian heard the gentle slumber of someone lying on his bed. He slowly walked up to the sound, gasping when he realized in the glow of the alarm clock light that it was the same girl. And she was not fully dressed.

Damian almost tripped over his own feet in the haste to exit, his face red enough to be a beacon in the dark. *Crap, crap, crap. I knocked. Please kill me now.* He had made it back out to the living area when he heard a sharp intake of breath. A few rustling and crashing sounds later, Mystery Girl was wearing one of his perfectly pressed and clean body-suits, modified to fit her slimmer figure. She had an electroshock blaster out and ready. Strapped to her hip just in case hung that oh-so-familiar knife.

"You promised me. Why did you break your promise?"

He saw the distrust in her eyes. Or was it just fear?

"Did you expect I could let you stay in my apartment forever?"

"I just needed another few days," she muttered, but her eyes refocused, angry and alert. "What did you see?"

"The lights weren't even on," Damian protested, backing away with hands held out in what he hoped was a non-threatening manner. "Nice electroshock gun by the way."

"Thanks, it's a new acquisition, but you didn't really answer my question."

Damian felt incredibly awkward, but the more he looked at the girl's face – her now clean face – and the more he saw her eyes slowly softening, the more he felt a little courage.

"Let's start over." He slowly walked forward, carefully dropping his bag first, until he was within easy strike of her electroshock gun. "My name is Damian Luxe. Your name is

Mystery Girl…sorry I couldn't be more original. Maybe you can help me with that? I can guess your name, if you want to make this an interactive game. Is it three syllables or two?"

He saw the ghost of a smile flash across her face. "You're kind of annoying."

"I'm hoping there's a 'but' coming right around the corner…"

"Vira." She gave him a half-decent grin now, and held out her hand to shake. The other hand was still gripping that electroshock gun for dear life.

"Pleasure to meet you, Vira." He gingerly took the hand, then was about to draw his hand back and gesture to the bag so he could give her a run-down of what he'd brought. That was when the whole place spiraled into chaos.

Damian had time to see her eyes cloud and shift into alarm. She dropped the electroshock gun as he whirled around, hearing the sounds of his door rebounding off the wall with a deafening crash. Three security androids burst into the room. The SA bots rushed into the living area, and before Damian knew what he was doing he had pinned Vira to the wall with his back, shielding her body with his.

The three humanoid robots blocked his escape on all sides. The middle android's visor-like face zoomed in with a loud whine as its neck extended.

"Citizen, I am Officer SA-3. Our patrol detected your door ajar and our records show that your key-print was used to access this living quarters while you were already clocked in for work at nightclub Twin Galaxies. This robot is not aware of any human who can exist in two places at once. Are you in duress, Citizen? Is this an intruder?"

Damian shook his head frantically, wanting to scream NO! The androids didn't read human body language well or pick up on verbal cues. But they weren't stupid either. They had a basis in rationality. If only he'd shut the stupid door...their programming forbade them to enter someone's personal living quarters without some physical sign for provocation.

The android tilted its head, then began to point at Vira. The girl's eyes were big pools of terror. Her heart was thundering in her chest, and Damian felt it through his body-suit. Dang it!

"Is this human a registered Citizen? All unregistered Citizens from lower sectors must have clearance. All illegals will be recycled, I repeat, all illegals will be recycled."

"She's not an illegal! She's my girlfriend, and we're both Citizens."

"We do not have her papers on file." The android waved at a small handheld console no bigger than the palm of a human hand.

"The papers are in processing! We submitted them not even an hour ago. She's from the outer sectors. The Haven AI had her escorted here, but there was an altercation with some illegals, and her escort had to be diverted. One of your own people later delivered the papers for her to sign and took them away. I swear it's true!"

He was lying through his teeth, but to an android it was possible that his story sounded convincing. Or so he hoped. Damian knew that if this encounter were happening in a public place things might go very differently. The SA bots often bulldozed first and asked questions later out on the street. But here in his apartment, which was technically his personal space, there were limits imposed on the SA bot's discretion.

His story was outlandish enough to make them skeptical, but he also knew for a fact that the rumors circulating about the Haven AI promoting people up from one sector to the next and, in rare cases, even up to Alpha Sector, had to have some basis in reality. He was gambling…with his life and hers.

The SA bots stared at him so long it made his skin crawl. Damian felt Vira's breath warm his neck, and it gave him a sense of comfort beyond what it had any right to.

"Are we done here?" he asked.

Crap. Why are they giving me that strange look?

Once in a while the SA bots seemed to take initiative rather than mindlessly follow their directives. Jenson had told him that the going theory was that their tiny AI sub-brains were evolving just like any living thing.

"We cannot verify this statement, Citizen, but our instructions classify this as a low-priority threat. I repeat, this is a low-priority threat. Give us some evidence proving your version of reality and we will leave the premises and discontinue our investigation."

"Give you...what?" Damian's mind was racing. He had made up a BS story. He didn't have any proof. One of the other SA bots reached for Vira.

Its manic, robotic voice droned. "Damian Luxe, please satisfy requested command or we will speak to this human female outside to verify. I repeat, please – "

"Hey, OK, OK, take it easy! Did I not tell you she was my girlfriend? Look, I'll prove it to you." Damian turned around, his whole body stiffening with tension. He mouthed the word K-I-S-S and gave her a frantic look that begged, 'Please don't go ballistic on me.'

Vira's gold-green eyes sharpened at first, relaxing with conscious effort. Vira let him lean forward, their lips touching. He felt the warmth of her breath, the softness of her body pressing against him for just those fleeting seconds as she entwined her arms around his neck to make it convincing enough even for human eyes. She deepened the kiss as Damian felt a protective urge consume his whole body. Suddenly his arms had gathered her tightly against his chest and the kiss found a life of its own.

It seemed an eternity later when they disengaged, her scent still clinging to him. The three security androids took a moment to process what had just happened.

SA3 finally piped up.

"These humans are exhibiting behavior consistent with Citizen Damian Luxe's prior assertion. I believe low-priority requirements have been met. Is this agreed?"

The other two security androids nodded and turned to lead the way out. Three seconds later the door slammed closed behind them, and Damian heard the beautiful music that was the lock mechanism sliding into place.

Vira and Damian sighed in unison. A loud smack echoed in the chamber as she slapped him. She picked up the electroshock blaster again and gave him a dirty look.

"There's not going to be an encore, buster."

Damian collapsed backward on the sofa and put both hands above his head. "I wouldn't dream of it. Give me a moment to get my heart rate back near something that won't make my chest explode. Then you can chew me out all you want, OK?"

Vira almost smiled. Once her own breathing finally slowed she sank down onto the couch a little distance from Damian's outstretched legs. Her sidelong look was wary but at least no longer lethal.

"So tell me…why did you really come here?"

With a deep breath Damian tried to decide. *Where do I start?*

Chapter 4

The Inner Fringe was not a place to be caught dead in. Damian's hand encircled Vira's much smaller one, but he was surprised to see her so perfectly calm. Like a willow tree smugly spitting into the teeth of an oncoming storm, she surveyed the dilapidation of the Inner Fringe with 'bring it on!' punctuating her every step. *But she's fragile too, just like the willow trees of Earth.* From birth Damian had been taught of the super-storms that had ravaged the world after human ingenuity 'fixing' climate change had only created a cure worse than the disease. He remembered watching film from old Earth when he was a boy, seeing a solitary willow tree which seemed to take all that the storm could hurl its way…until a final gust ripped it out by its roots.

That's not going to happen to you or your girl, dude. Don't be so dramatic. Wondering if Jenson had somehow invaded his mind with telepathic disapproval, Damian glanced back and saw his friend moving discreetly in the distance. Wearing the Dumbledoor suit, he stuck out like a very sore thumb in a shantytown where rags and half-nakedness were the norm. The Haven AI called this the Inner Fringe, but citizens of Beta Sector had another name for it. The "Intestines."

The ones who dwelled here were outcasts, thieves, criminals, political dissidents, and anyone else who hadn't known when to stop or shut up until it was too late. The authorities liquidated some of them, but the very reputation of the place served another purpose to Damian's frame of mind. Why kill those who were opposed to the good things the AI was doing, giving criminals an easy way out? Justice could be more poetic than that. No, instead the AI let them wallow in their own filth in a crazy-glued society where murder, rape, and killing for a thimble of water were as common as 'Please' and 'Thank you' up above. What better way to prove to the people of Beta Sector what would happen if the Crew of Alpha Sector and the Haven AI were no longer allowed to guide the generations' future?

Yes, but you aren't playing the good citizen now, are you? You're not supposed to be here, dumbass. Damian shoved that thought as far back into his head as it would go.

"So...not to complain. You are, I guess, putting your butt on the line for me...but how are we getting back into the city if something goes wrong?" Vira asked.

"We should have three hours until the authorities find the new passage that the black marketers just tunneled. If we don't get back in time, my contact told me that this," he stopped, holding up a tiny holo-view attached to the underside of his forearm, "will give us directions to an alternate route."

"And what makes you so sure that this genetic freak buddy of yours who lives in the shadows won't just let us all rot out here?"

"At least two reasons," Damian replied with an easy grin. "He doesn't get the second half of his payment until we get back safely, #1. And #2, Jenson and I have a mutual friend who dabbles in the black market and knows where said genetic freak operates. Our mutual friend is not the sort of person you want to anger, unless having four limbs seems a burden to you."

Vira wrinkled her nose. "Such a typical guy. Do all of your analogies have to be based on physical violence?"

"Nope. Only the most fun ones."

They were walking along a tall, narrow tunnel with shanty houses built partly on stilts and huddling against the rock walls anywhere from one to three stories up. Lichen grew on the roofs, the staple crop for anyone eking out an existence where little else of nutritional value could sustain itself. It felt more like walking through a rat-infested den than a settlement, and the stench at times was just about as bad.

"I've grown up fearing the SA bots. It feels weird not seeing them patrol," Vira admitted. "But this seems almost worse. It's creepy."

Damian glanced at Vira. She wore a padded vest and fatigue pants to protect her well enough from knife attacks, but a sharp projectile would still skewer her, and her face was unprotected. He felt only marginally better when he took the time to admire the two long knives and six-set throwing knives buckled to her hips and waist.

"Are you even listening to me or are you checking out my figure?" Vira growled.

"Don't flatter yourself," Damian grunted. It had been five days since the SA bot scare in his apartment. Five days they'd had to prepare for this reckless scheme to get Vira the fake papers she needed. But it already seemed like a lifetime had passed between them, and Damian found himself relaxed around her, even under pressure. Especially under pressure.

"I was just thinking that I'd much rather *you* were wearing the exosuit and I was wearing the black get-up."

"Yeah, well, last time I checked bulky exosuits custom-fitted for broad-shouldered males don't exactly do it for me. I prefer having other abilities…like *being able to walk.*"

Damian sighed. They had had this argument a hundred times. Refitting the exosuit for her wouldn't have been impossible. Expensive? Yes. Time-consuming? Yes. As annoying as a bad bowel movement? Almost certainly. Jenson had taken her side in the argument, and that had been that.

The main thoroughfare of the Inner Fringe was called "The Gut," and they followed it for what seemed like eight or nine kilometers. A few souls peeked out at them from between the slats of boarded-up windows. Garbage littered the tunnel-cum-street. Every now and then the all-seeing eyes of a camera perched at the top of the corridor looked down on them, shielded with projectile-proof glass. Random video-feed of the Inner Fringe was broadcast to citizens of Beta Sector. It was currently the most popular running show you could view on the casts, a lot like the mindless "reality" programs of old Earth.

Damian and Vira came to a stop at the first major intersection. The thoroughfare opened out into three major corridors, and a fourth smaller corridor tunneled through the rock. Damian pointed at a graffiti symbol sprayed in red depicting a skull and a prosthesis-augmented human body.

"There. That's our subtle hint. We go down that minor tunnel." From the corner of his eye, he saw Vira flinch.

"You look like you just saw a ghost," he said.

"No, it's just...I've seen that symbol before," she replied.

His eyebrows went up, but he left it alone. They didn't have time to hash it out. Focusing on the poorly lit corridor ahead, Damian drew out his phosphorescent beacon. Made from chemicals extracted from genetically modified insects, it bathed the room in an eerie blue-green glow. It also prevented Damian from stepping headlong into a 20-foot drop as the corridor widened into a huge chamber. He threw his free arm out, preventing Vira from tipping over the edge. Looking more cautiously, he saw a ladder attached to the side of the precipice. The lower ground ran for perhaps 40 to 50 yards before another ladder, this one twice as long as the first, ran up to a towering ledge that overlooked the whole area.

"I'd like to say a few choice words right about now," Damian muttered.

"I'm sure they'd be colorful," Vira replied, giving his hand a short squeeze. "But if I were you, I wouldn't try the ladder. It doesn't look the sturdiest, and the added weight of your exosuit might get us both killed. Better if I go by myself from here."

Damian's eyes bulged. "Not in a million eons." Then he grinned as he estimated the drop one more time. "You don't know much about exosuits, do you?"

Vira gave him a glare that said 'Why should I?'.

"Hold on TIGHT," Damian growled.

Vira found him pulling her behind him by the wrist. He gave her time to notice the two easy hand-holds where the exosuit harness circled around his back so that she could mount up. Atop his bulky exosuit she looked a little like a girl getting a piggy-back ride.

"If you get us killed I'm coming back to haunt your friend Jenson," Vira muttered. Then Damian imagined her stomach doing a flip as he launched them over the edge. The rush of air made Damian glad she'd tied up her hair into a ponytail. With a crash they landed on a pile of plastic and cardboard debris. Vira shuddered and hopped off, obviously only too glad to have solid rock under her feet again.

"You're a menace," she panted. "You could give a girl a little more time to prepare herself before hurling us down a black hole."

Damian was too busy checking their surroundings to smile. This little dip in geography was prime real estate for ambushes. The ledge overlooking it was also a perfect place for projectile-launched surprises.

A tall, lone figure approached from the shadows.

"Welcome. I am Mr. Jin, and I will be your guide." The dark-skinned stranger had a handsome, rugged face and easy-to-trust eyes. The hair on the back of Damian's neck snapped to alertness.

"We've come to pick up the papers from Madame D," Damian replied. "Where is she?"

"I will take you to her," Mr. Slick-and-tall replied. Wearing a skin-tight black body-suit, this so-called guide was the best dressed person they'd yet seen. Pretty much the only person they'd seen, Damian reminded himself.

The two cautiously followed. Damian's steps echoed in the corridor as he crushed random rubble and empty ampoules underfoot. He latched the beacon glow-globe to his shoulder, giving himself two free hands in case things got suspicious.

Mr. Jin led them down a side hallway that broke away where the tiny canyon petered out. Damian carefully memorized the maze of turns which Mr. Jin took them down, and realized with a sickening lurch that the chances of Jenson keeping up were slimming by the second.

Finally they entered an open conference room with a raised platform at the end. The room had an official feel to it.

Damian sensed that this was where deals were made and back stabs fulfilled.

"Are you two…?" Mr. Jin let the question hang. Vira and Damian shook heads at the same time.

"Not that it's any of your business, Mr. Tall, Dark, and Creepy. I want to see Madame D now and I want to see the papers I've already paid for," Damian snarled. He swung around, his fist reaching for Mr. Jin's neck. The air around Mr. Jin shimmered suddenly, the camo-cloaking field vanishing as Mr. Jin's entire torso seemed to bulge outward. He was wearing an exosuit! *Urth it to the Bowels. Son of a…*

The dark-skinned face smiled as his metal-sheathed fist slammed into the side of Damian's head. Damian tried to stay upright, but the sheer force threw him into the wall. He heard many footsteps as six more figures leapt down from the stage. He heard Mr. Jin bellow in pain as Vira's throwing knife found his neck, slipping through the exosuit's defenses.

Mr. Jin staggered back, holding a hand to the wound. His eyes became unfocused and he lurched to his knees. Damian had righted himself now, looking in awe at the homeless girl he thought could handle herself reasonably well. Correction. Kick butt and take names, apparently.

A woman darted in to intervene, stretching her hands palm outward with an imperious air, her eyes flicking between Damian and Vira. "Not bad. Jin's one of my best. He's never failed to block a thrown weapon…until now." Her face suddenly shined with a radiant smile, but Damian wasn't fooled. He looked at Vira, saw determination mixed with…something he couldn't quite put his finger on. She looked like she wanted answers.

"I didn't think it took seven people to make a simple hand-off of papers," Vira replied drily. She looked pointedly at the two men nearest her, each with prosthetic limbs and hard faces. They carried themselves like bruisers.

Three more men in disheveled coats and masks carried electroshock blasters, and had already fanned out behind them to block any exit.

The woman who appeared to be their leader gave a reassuring grin. "You have nothing to fear from me, Vira. You are Vira, am I correct?"

The girl slowly nodded. "And who's wanting to know?"

"I am Madame D," the woman replied. "I know you've come for papers, and I have papers," she continued, waving a syringe in her free hand. 'Papers' weren't literally papers. That was the code word used by criminals for what was needed to get a new identity.

It was in your DNA. The system looked for certain markers when you went to work, no matter the occupation, or if you were detained by the SA bots in search of a high-risk fugitive, to identify you as an upstanding citizen. It was like a safety blanket that every citizen had…and those without it lived in constant fear.

"Forgive my man, Vira. I fear he was offended by your lack of trust, bringing this exosuited bruiser bodyguard with you when we could just as easily have handled this like civilized people." Damian didn't detect a single note of sincerity in the woman's voice.

"Shall we get this over with?" Madame D asked.

Vira nodded and sat in the nearest chair. She unbuttoned her padded sleeve and rolled it up, exposing the veins. "I'm game if you are. If you or your men try something, I think you'll be impressed by how dangerous my companion can be." Vira gave Damian a nod, and Damian quickly positioned himself in the center of the room near Vira's side.

He was surrounded, yes, but he was now ready for the next attack. He'd had to turn off his force field crystal before making the leap into the canyon...now he unobtrusively activated it. Go ahead, try that again. Punch me again, dumbass, and see what happens.

Mr. Jin had already drawn out the knife in his neck and slapped a heal-patch over it. The patch thrummed as it did its work, reknitting flesh and sealing the wound. With a hiss of satisfaction Mr. Jin stretched out the muscles in his back and strode up beside Madame D. The two pairs stood face to face now, tension coiling through the air.

"This may sting a bit," Madame D. replied, smiling. She injected the needle perfectly, pushing the syringe until the DNA-replication solution was fully infused into Vira's body.

Damian didn't want to know which poor soul they'd kidnapped from Beta Sector, extracted DNA from, and killed to create this fake and untraceable identity.

That was when all hell broke loose and decided to dance a jig.

The process of incorporating the new DNA markers should have been painless. Instead, Vira's body began to writhe, her eyes going wild as she slumped suddenly in her chair. At the same time Mr. Jin lunged at Damian. Damian's exosuit flared with bright, blue light as the force field activated. Jin's eyes grew wide with shock as Damian's well-aimed fist punched through the man's exosuit faceplate, crushing his skull with a sickening crack as Damian's hand flared with the same blue flash. Damian turned as Mr. Jin sagged backward like a discarded puppet.

But the two prosthesis-armed men had already pulled Vira from the chair and spread her out over the table. One of them grasped Vira by the neck and looked over at Damian's anguished face.

Madame D calmly stroked her lips as if deep in thought.

"I wonder if you can get to her before his arm breaks her neck. Oh wait…I think that question has an easy answer."

She looked at him, no longer smiling. "The ball is in your court, Damian."

"How do you know my name?"

"Your genetic freak friend didn't tell you? I always do research on my potential customers. And your Vira...now she's a special customer indeed."

"What are you talking about?"

"I can do this one of two ways. It would be better if Vira were alive, but she can be just as useful to me dead. You're going to power down that exosuit and let my men take you out of it."

"The hell I am."

"Or...you're going to get the girl you love killed."

"Love? Look, I don't care what you do with her," Damian lied. "But with this exosuit I can break your neck like a twig. And I will. So make *your* choice. Release us both or die."

Madame D considered those heated words for several long seconds. Damian could be a good liar when he wanted to. But Damian also feared that his facial expressions had already given him away. *I don't love her, dang it.* He liked Vira, though. He had only met her a few weeks ago, and he already liked her. A lot.

Damian's heart sank as he realized that Madame D had just come to the same conclusion.

"Bruce, if he moves I want you to break her neck."

Damian tensed up, ready to spring. He looked at Vira's relaxed face, her helpless body and the delicate neck that would be all too easy to snap.

"OK! OK! Urth it all. Take it easy! Don't hurt her."

Damian felt the hope spill out of him until his mind was running on despair. He deactivated the Vuldemort exosuit and let his limbs go lifeless. A few minutes later and the three masked guards on Madame D's team had extricated him from his only weapon. He wore only his gray-and-black body-suit underneath. Madame D produced another liquid-filled syringe and approached as two of the guards extended his arm, rolled up the sleeve, and held it still.

"This may prick, just a little." Damian thought about struggling, even now. That was instinct talking.

"Don't struggle, Damian...if I'd wanted to kill you, you'd be dead," Madame D said, her voice almost cheerful.

Damian looked straight into those midnight-black eyes framed by the tumble of stormy blond, brown, and black highlights of hair. Madame D looked like a cyber-witch from hell.

"You'll forgive me for saying I don't exactly trust you," he mumbled, as the needle lanced his flesh and the drug did its work. The world clouded, dimmed, and then was no more...

#####

End of *Part One* - Don't miss the complete novel of

Crysalis: Vira's Tale

For availability check J. Kirsch's Smashwords author page or Amazon.

#####

You can also check J. Kirsch's Amazon page or Smashwords Author page to find his action-packed *Tales from Omega Station* stories, adventures set in a dangerous world on the edge of known space.

WHAT IS OMEGA STATION?

Omega Station, aka the Rock. A barren, airless asteroid on the outermost edge of the galaxy, home of the richest of the rich and the poorest of the poor. Dotted with commercial, military and residential domes, the outer surface is the place to live for those who can afford it or are lucky enough to work there.

But the vast majority of the Rock's residents don't live in the surface domes; instead, they have tunneled downwards, moving ever further towards its fiery heart. The upper levels are safe, comfortable, secure—or as secure as anyone can be on Omega Station. The lower levels, now; they are home to the detritus of a double dozen races and species, all living in uneasy juxtaposition, fighting, loving, eating—and being eaten.

The Rock's location in space, the last real port before exiting the galaxy, has made it a valuable commodity to many governments and private corporations, as has the addictive drug straz, which grows only in its recycling vats. Control has been taken and given in a hundred bloody battles over the years, but those who live in the lower levels—and further down, in the Depths—are often barely aware of whoever claims to be in charge.

No one, really, rules the Rock, whatever they may claim, however many weapons and warriors they throw against it.

For the Rock is eternal…and it has many stories…

Acknowledgments

I would like to thank loved ones, friends, and others who helped me on the way:

My better half, B. - Thank you for being my adventuring partner in crime, inspirer, and fellow dreamer. You are amazing.

My parents, who taught me how to dream in the first place.

Gail, Jim, C. J., Cory, Adam, and all the other authors who gave me a nudge in the right direction or were generous about lending me some of their creative fuel.

Finally, and certainly not least, a big 'Thank You!' to every librarian who ever encouraged me to pick up a good book and to every reader who has given me helpful feedback. It has been worth more to me than gold.

About the Author of *Princess*:

J. Kirsch is a member of the Science Fiction & Fantasy Writers of America. As a librarian he promotes fantasy and science fiction to readers of all stripes, usually with excellent results. He writes about strong heroines who face tough obstacles and work with what they have, often using humor as a deadly weapon. He tells stories where friendship, love, personal resilience and a little ruthless pragmatism are all parts of survival. In his fantasy novels sometimes that involves destroying six-eyed monsters, cruel sorcerers, or the occasional vengeful imp, but this is by no means an exhaustive list.

Sometimes, as one of J. Kirsch's favorite authors once noted, fantasy and science fiction uniquely explore the very kinds of problems people face every day.

A Few Other Tidbits...

J. lives and adventures in the Carolinas with a fearless spouse and noticeably cute canine. He has always enjoyed storytelling, perhaps thanks to the two librarians who raised him on a steady diet of imagination.

J. enjoys writing in all genres of fiction, but fantasy, science fiction, and adventure stories will always be his passions (sometimes with a healthy dose of romance). You can find information on J.'s latest projects on his blog, **Starfarers and Knights**, or by viewing his **Smashwords Author Page**.

40091461R00144

Made in the USA
Lexington, KY
24 March 2015